MY
RECKLESS
EARL

TAMARA Gill

COPYRIGHT

MY RECKLESS EARL, The Wayward Woodvilles, Book 7 ©
2022 by Tamara Gill
Cover Art by Wicked Smart Designs
Editor Grace Bradley Editing, LLC

ISBN: 978-0-6457257-7-3 (trade paperback)

ONE

London Season, 1811

Harlow York took a fortifying breath and entered Lord and Lady Craig's conservatory. She prayed she was not about to walk in on Lord Kemsley in the throes of passion with some other random debutante or widow of the *ton*.

She closed her eyes a moment, pausing on the threshold of the room, and sent up a silent prayer that her worst nightmare would not come to pass. The scent of the hot house seemed more potent when one took a moment to close one's eyes to the room's physical beauty.

The scents of wisteria, roses, and citrus trees filled her senses, and she breathed deep, stepping into the room.

"I would ask you what you're doing at the

doors to this conservatory looking as if you're about to faint, but I will not. Instead, I will merely ask you why do you have your eyes closed and why are you following me, Miss York?" The deep baritone of Lord Kemsley drifted from the shadows of the vast, glass room.

Harlow swallowed her nerves, ignored his strange commentary on her closed eyes, and started in the direction she believed he stood.

"I came to speak to you, Lord Kemsley. I hope I have not interrupted you."

He stepped out of the shadow of a large orange tree, and so too did the widow Randall. The blush on the dowager's cheeks told Harlow without words how they had occupied themselves in their few minutes alone.

"I apologize. I did not know you were not alone."

"And nor should you ever know that," Lady Randall cooed, running her hand along Lord Kemsley's chest before sauntering past Harlow. "But do not worry, Miss York. Your secret is safe with me so long as mine is safe with you."

Harlow nodded and fought not to cast up her accounts. He had a lover? A woman who was not Harlow. Pain shot through her chest, and she fisted her hands at her sides to stop herself from stomping her foot at the unfairness of it all.

"What can I help you with, Miss York?" he drawled, lighting a cheroot and walking to her, towering over her like the god she had always believed him to be.

She stopped herself from sighing at how lovely he was, even knowing he had lovers. Of course, a man like Lord Kemsley shared his bed with society women who did not need husbands. Such as the lucky widow Lady Randall.

He was a man, and he could do as he wished.

But would he do as Harlow wished?

"I need your assistance, my lord," she managed, glad her voice came out determined and not shaky with undecidedness. "I've come here tonight to ask for it."

He breathed deep into his cheroot, his eyes narrowing as the smoke wafted past his eyes. "My help? Really?" He paused, chewing his bottom lip. "What does the Season's diamond require with my help? I would not think you were in need of any."

"I'm no longer the diamond. Miss Marshall has been named this year's incomparable, and I'm very happy for her. And more than happy to relinquish my title, for it would only get in the way of what I want this year."

He raised his brow, staring down at her over his straight, aristocratic nose. "Do explain."

Harlow nodded. This was it, the time she would say her piece and hope for the best. What was the worst that could happen?

He could say no and laugh you out of this room.

She pushed the horrible thought aside and promised herself it would all be well. He was not a mean man. He may be one of London's most debauched rogues, but he was never so bedeviled as not to dance with and say pretty words to the young ladies who crossed his path each Season.

Although she did not know his age, he could not be so much older than her elder sister Lila.

"You see, my lord, I'm in love with a man who does not love me in return. In fact, there are times when I do not think he even knows that I exist, but I want to change that truth."

"Really?" he said, his lips twitching and showing the first sign of amusement, and not annoyance, at her interrupting him. "And how is seeking me out going to help you with this love interest of yours?"

"Well ..." She gulped. "I want you to show me how I, as a young woman who has so much to learn, may understand what I need to do to make the gentleman I admire see me."

"You want my tutelage on the art of courtship?" He frowned, shaking his head. "You want me to help you speak to his lordship? I'm not certain I understand."

"Well, a conversation is certainly a factor that I shall need to get better at, but there are other things too. Other things that a man may like a woman to be well-versed in that would help his lordship see me as something other than another debutante looking for a good match."

Harlow stared at him, hoping he would not make her say what she feared he understood but still played ignorant of.

"Such as?" he asked again, the grin on his lips now a full, wicked smile.

"Such as," she started, clearing her throat. Heat kissed her cheeks, and she licked her lips, looking anywhere but at Lord Kemsley's smug visage. "Such as in the ways of seduction. How I may saunter near my intended. Coy looks or touches when we speak. Maybe even a kiss or two," she suggested.

His deep, guttural chuckle made the hairs on the back of her neck stand on end, and not in a terrifying way. "You want me to teach you how to seduce the man of your heart?"

Harlow nodded, unable to voice a reply.

"Well, that is bold of you, Miss York. I did not think a little mouse from Grafton would have such plans for a lord of the realm, but how mistaken I am."

"I understand if you do not wish to proceed, my lord. And if you do not, I ask that you not share my plans with my family or friends. They would not understand or approve."

He studied her a moment, and she wondered what he saw when he looked at her. A woman of sun-kissed hair. A woman with a mole above her lip and freckles on her nose after spending too much time outdoors these past weeks after the cold winter. She was not usually one to spend time in the garden, but being back in Grafton during the winter, the few warm weeks before they returned to London, she longed to be outdoors. Freckles, unfortunately, were an occupational hazard when one sits and plots how to win a rogue's heart.

Lord Kemsley's heart, to be exact ...

WES WAS A LITTLE FOXED. IN FACT, FOR A moment, he thought the delectable Miss York was an apparition sprung from his inebriation that had formed before him, asking him to do all kinds of mischief.

But how wrong he was.

She was not a figment of his imagination. She was very real and very much asking him to teach her how to seduce some unknown gentleman in London this Season.

He thought her antics with his good friend Viscount Billington last Season had been outrageous, but how wrong he was. The woman had no end to her plots and plans.

"How far will this teaching of mine go, Miss York? You know I'm a rake, which I'm certain is why you've singled me out, but how far do you wish to take your lessons?" he asked, calling the chit's bluff. She would not go too far. She was a maid, after all. Pure and untouchable, as all of them were. She would not allow him to kiss her, so her teachings would be dull indeed.

But then he inwardly shrugged. That may still secure her a match. There were certainly enough boring, staid gentlemen in town who did not mind a frigid wife.

She swallowed, biting her bottom lip, and he took a deep breath. The younger Miss York had always caught his attention. There was something mischievous about her that he had always marveled at. Her escapades with his good friend last Season confirmed those suspicions.

"As I said, my lord, I will require teachings on what I should speak about when we dance, what touches or looks work on you that may work on my mystery gentleman. I cannot fail at winning the man I want, so I shall need to know if there is any time that a woman, an unmarried woman such as myself, should offer more than light flirtation." She paused, biting that delectable lip again and his vision of her swam. "I would like to know if there is any time I ought to offer my lips to the gentleman."

Wes swallowed. Hard. This was not the sort of conversation he ought to be having as foxed as he was. "You want me to kiss you?"

"What!" she gasped, her eyes growing wide.

"No, well ..." she hedged. "Not yet, at least, but maybe a little into our lessons."

Wes closed his eyes, his cock twitching at the thought of taking Miss York's lips, even if solely due to lessons in seduction she was asking for. He wasn't sure he could stop at one kiss if Harlow York was in his arms.

"I do not think it is a good idea," he said, glad that the little bit of gentlemanly caution had stepped forward and forced those words out of his mouth. "I'm a rake, and if you're caught anywhere alone with me, such as you are now, marriage will be to me, and no one else, and I do not think that is what you want. Correct me if I'm wrong," he demanded of her.

She opened her mouth as if to say something but snapped it closed. "You could teach me in secret. No one needs to know. I trust you because you are my brother-in-law's friend, and my sister holds you in great esteem. I know you will not hurt me or overstep your bounds. I will be safe with you, my lord."

Wes stared at Miss York, unsure if he wanted to laugh hysterically at her words and prove her wrong or spend a few enjoyable weeks teaching her before walking away once she secured the man she desired.

He debated the pros and cons of her plan and blinked when she wobbled before him again. He really ought to make a decision with a clear head, not right now when he was foxed.

"Please, my lord," she said beseechingly, coming up to him and taking his hands, squeezing them in appeal. "Please do not turn me away."

"It is a dangerous game you play, Miss York. Are you certain you're up for my teachings?" he asked, wanting to give her one last out should she want it.

Her eyes brightened to a vibrant green, and the pit of his stomach clenched. "I want you and no one else, my lord."

He pulled his hands free and nodded. "Very well then. Let the teachings begin." And God help them both they survived them.

Two

Harlow tapped her foot at the Daniels' ball and surreptitiously watched the ballroom doors for Lord Kemsley's arrival. The earl was famous for arriving late and leaving early, but he had promised to help her, and they would start her instruction tonight.

The fact his lordship did not know his teachings were aimed to win his heart and no one else's was a precious little secret just for her, and for him to find out.

In time.

Nerves fluttered in her stomach, and she fought to keep her features poised and not bursting with excitement at being able to spend the evening with his lordship. To have him guide her, pretending to make the man she admired jealous of their association. To help her hone her seductive wiles for the use on the man teaching her instead.

The plan could not be any more perfect, but she dared not share it with anyone, not even her sister, whom she was staying with this Season. Lila was beyond helping with any more scandalous ideas that Harlow came up with, and she would be determined to stop her plan should she know of it.

Her heart lurched at Lord Kemsley entering the ballroom, his tall, athletic build catching the eye of herself and other debutantes. Not to mention several widows, the widow Randall no exception to his charms.

Harlow ground her teeth, hating the idea of any competition for Lord Kemsley's attention, not to mention affections. She wanted him to be hers and no one else's. And thanks to his agreeing to help her secure her imaginary gentleman, she would be able to occupy his time more than anyone else.

He strode through the throng of guests, oblivious to the dreamy expressions of the women he passed. His wavy blond hair made him look like a sun-kissed god, and her fingers twitched, eager to run through those golden locks.

He caught sight of her, and his expression changed to one of determination, and she sucked in a breath, having not expected to feel all at sea when his attention settled on her.

"Miss York," he said, bowing before her. He

picked up her hand and kissed the top of her silk glove before meeting her eyes.

Harlow swallowed and fought to find words that would not come out like a squeaky mouse caught in a trap. "Lord Kemsley, how delightful it is to see you this evening. What brings you to my side of the ballroom?" she asked, keeping the conversation light and respectable.

A wicked light flickered in his blue eyes. "I thought you may like to dance with me, Miss York. Please tell me your card is not full, and I have missed my opportunity already?" he asked, loud enough for others to hear.

She chuckled, handing him her wrist so he could write on her dance card. "Of course not, my lord. There is always room for you," she replied, grinning.

He smiled as he wrote his name on two different dances, and Harlow fought to school her features so as not to look like a woman who wanted to holler and bounce before the *ton*.

She thought that he may make his excuses and leave her until their dance, but instead, he came and stood beside her, looking about them to ensure their privacy.

"So, you wish to learn how to ensure your chosen gentleman finally notices you and makes the appropriate moves to win your heart."

Harlow nodded. "Yes, that is right. But then I need to know what I should do when he does to ensure he knows that I'm interested and welcoming of his suit."

"Very well, that should be simple enough." He cast his attention on the room. "Is he here this evening?" he asked her.

"Yes, and not far away, so do be your charming self and help me make him notice your interest."

"That I'm standing beside you and I'm not in the gaming room with several gentlemen friends makes it obvious I'm interested in you," he quipped, meeting her eyes.

A delicious warmth spread through her body at his words, and she had to remind herself this was all a game. His being his charming self. Not that he really thought the things he was conveying.

"Thank you for assisting me, my lord. I'm hopeful that your lessons will not be in vain."

"So do I, and I hope you shall invite me to the wedding," he asked her, a teasing note in his voice.

"I should imagine your attendance will be necessary after all of our efforts," she returned. And if her little plan worked, he would not only be at the wedding, but beside her when she was before the priest.

"Very good, for I do enjoy the wedding breakfasts afterward," he stated, taking two glasses of champagne from a passing footman and handing her one.

"What would you like your first lesson to be, Miss York? I'm yours to command."

"Well," she said, taking a fortifying sip. "We shall dance, and I think you ought to hold me close, maybe a little closer than is proper, but not so much that you cause offense or talk about the town. Although I'm sure the talk will come no matter what since you're to single me out more over the next few weeks before I secure my offer of marriage."

His attention slid over her body, and Harlow felt his inspection of her like a physical caress. His eyes lingered on her bosom before dipping to her hips and then right down to her silk-slippered toes. The man was a walking lure of everything sexual and naughty, all things a woman such as she was ought not to know but did. She knew a lot more than he would ever believe.

Since her sister's marriage, Harlow had access to Lord Billington's libraries here in London and at his country estate. Those libraries were filled with books not meant for innocent young lady's eyes, such as herself, but upon finding them, she had devoured every one.

Lord Kemsley's tutelage would be a confirmation more than the instruction of what she had learned, and she could not wait to begin. To feel alive, wanted, and experience the desire she had read of in its physical form, manifested within her own body and soul.

To be more blunt, she could not wait for him to touch her ...

WES BEAT DOWN HIS RAKISH URGES THAT seemed to raise their naughty heads each time he looked upon Miss York. That his student, as he now would term her, had a delectable body, an angelic face, and lips of sin did not help the matter of keeping his hands to himself. One could lose themselves in her fierce, green eyes, which lingered upon a person as if they could read one's mind.

Hell, he hoped she could not read his.

But then, she did not want him to keep his hands away from her, not entirely, which made his teaching of her even more problematic.

How would he ever behave without getting entangled in a situation neither of them wanted?

She had her heart set on another, whom he would love to know the identity of, but he doubted she would reveal such a truth. He tore his gaze from her, looking about the room and studying the young men present tonight.

Not many were appealing, not to his eye in any case, but then his interests did not lay in that direction.

They lay in the feminine kind, like the one at his side.

"I think I can do as you ask, and I will give you instructions as we go that will help increase your chances of gaining your beau's attention."

"That would be wonderful, my lord," she said, her eyes alight with excitement.

He grinned just as the musicians started the first notes of the waltz. "Shall we, my dear?" he asked her, holding out his arm.

She nodded, entwining her arm with his, and he led her out onto the ballroom floor before pulling her into his arms.

She was all womanly curves. Her hips flared at the perfect angle, the cut of her gown giving tantalizing glimpses of her breasts. She glanced at him as they moved into the dance, swaying and spinning down the room. "When we're together such as we are now, keep looking at me. Meet my eye, and do not let it shift. We must appear to be besotted with each other, no one else."

"Like this, my lord?" She met his eyes, holding his gaze with a steely determination that made the pit of his gut clench. Ladies of sensitive, delicate natures should not know how to look upon a man such as Miss York was looking upon him, but here he was, with such a lady under his instruction and feeling all at sea by the way she watched him.

As if she knew something he did not. Was

privy to some delectable secret he was unaware of.

Was she?

"The way you're looking at me may even fool me, Miss York," he stated, having never said anything truer in his life. When Miss York wanted to play at being interested in someone, she did it very well.

"Well, we are friends now, I hope, and I do like you, so it is easy for me to pretend that we shall one day be husband and wife. Lovers, in fact."

Wes tripped on his feet and was only stopped from landing flat on his face by Miss York holding his arm and halting his fall. He cleared his throat, looking about the room and hoping the *ton* had not seen his faux pas.

"You are very direct with your words, Miss York."

She chuckled, slipping back into his arms and the dance. He watched her, moving by instinct, and marveled at her grace.

"It's all a game, my lord. No harm or insinuation in my words. You're just a good teacher, that is all."

"True, I'm very apt at the game of seduction and pretend."

The light in her eyes dimmed at his words before she seemed to shake off her melancholy and smiled at him. "What else can we do to appear besotted? He is watching me now," she said.

He pulled her close as they moved in a circular motion. He dipped his hand low on her back, his fingers sliding upon her lithe, firm body beneath her silk gown. Without thinking, he pulled her closer still, so much so that he could feel the front of her body.

Her mouth opened in a silent gasp, and he fought for control. What was happening here? Why was he so overcome with desire for the woman in his arms?

She was a maid, a woman looking for a husband. Had, in fact, picked out one and was trying to lure him in with another man's assistance.

He did not want to tup the woman in his arms and have her first, only to let her go later.

That would never do. He may be a rake, but even he had a line he would not cross. Not even with the darling, naughty Miss Harlow York.

THREE

The dance came to an unfortunate end, and Harlow was surprised at how quickly Lord Kemsley walked her back to her sister and made his excuses before leaving.

She watched him, back ramrod straight and head held high as he made his way through the crowded ballroom before she lost sight of him.

"What are you up to this year, Harlow?" Lila asked her, one curious brow raised high on her forehead.

"Nothing," Harlow answered, schooling her features to look serene and innocent. Not that she could look all that innocent. Not after the dance she had just had with Lord Kemsley.

He had pulled her so close that she could feel things. A hard, long, something in his breeches she should not have. That she had brushed it more than once on purpose—taking a little hint from one of the books she had read, which stated such a thing was what men liked at times—had not been met with disappointment.

If anything, his lordship had seemed a little at sea from what she was making him feel, and that was just where she wanted him to be—in her hand like clay, perfect for forming and sculpting her every desire and dream.

"It did not look like nothing," Lila stated. "He seemed very taken with you all of a sudden." Lila glanced in the direction Lord Kemsley had walked. "Why is that, do you think, when you thought him so disinterested in you last Season?"

Harlow shrugged. "I could not tell you, but we know each other better now that you're married to Lord Billington. They are friends, after all."

"Hmm," Lila said, and nothing else before her husband joined them and swept her out onto the dance floor.

Harlow breathed a sigh of relief, looking for her favorite friend Lady Leigh. She spotted Isla across the room and started toward her, joining her small group of friends a moment later.

Isla smiled and beckoned her when she caught sight of her. "Harlow, I'm so glad you're here. I have missed you since we parted last Season."

Harlow kissed her friend's cheek and dipped into a curtsy. "I have missed you also. How was your time in the country? Did you enjoy being away from town?"

"Oh yes, it was perfect in every way," Isla said with a wistful tone. Something that often happened whenever she spoke of her husband Viscount Leigh and their life together. But Harlow supposed that is what happens when one fell in love and made such a beautiful match.

She prayed that she, too, would have a marriage just so. If she could convince Lord Kemsley that he no longer wanted to be a bachelor but instead a husband. Hers, to be exact.

"Walk with me," Isla said, pulling her from the small set of ladies. "I saw you dancing with Lord Kemsley. Does this mean you've spoken to him, and he has agreed to your plans?"

Harlow had written to Isla during the winter to let her know her plans and hopes. Isla had cautioned her but promised to help her in any way, should she need it.

"I did. I asked him as I said I would at the Craig's ball the other evening, and after a little to-and-fro, Lord Kemsley agreed to help me."

Isla's eyes widened, and she fought not to grin. "Well, that is promising. I would not think any gentleman would help a lady unless there was some degree of interest. Do you not think?"

"That is what I'm hoping," Harlow said. "He's promised to dance with me twice, be a little too familiar with me during those times to try to make my pretend intended interested in me more."

"It truly is a brilliant plan, and if he does not step forward and declare himself in love with you by the end of the Season, then he did not ever deserve you in the first place."

"Agreed," Harlow stated, nodding. "And no one is hurt in this little game I play. Other than myself if he does not fall in love with me."

"That is only true if he does not find out about your plan." Isla pulled her to a stop and met her eye. "What if the worst happens and he does not give up his rakish ways to settle down with you? What will you do? How far are you willing to take this game? I caution you only because I do not want you to see yourself ruined by a gentleman, even one we like as much as we do if he will not marry you at the end of it all."

Isla made a good point, which she had mulled over for many weeks. What if, during one of their lessons, their arrangement got out of hand and his tutelage was taken too far? If that happened, then any hope of a good match would be gone forever. How could she marry another when she had been improper with a different man before marriage? How could she marry another when her stubborn heart refused to give up hope on Lord Kemsley?

"I must trust and hope with everything that I am that this ploy of mine will work and that

Lord Kemsley will fall in love with me before the end of the Season. The alternative is not something I want to imagine."

Isla frowned, the concern her friend felt clear on her visage. "Well, how he looked at you tonight, surely that could not all be acting. Deep down, I believe he desires you, which is the first step in building a foundation with his lordship."

"Did you desire Lord Leigh before you loved him?" Harlow asked.

Isla chuckled. "You know I disliked Lord Leigh before I liked him very much. So many things can happen when dislike goes up against desire. Desire wins out every time, Harlow, and I believe that will be the case with you and Lord Kemsley too."

"Oh, I do hope you are right." A footman passed with ratafia, and Harlow procured two glasses, handing one to Isla. "I'm hoping to make him so passionately in love with me that any lady who would once have turned his head will fade by comparison to what I can offer him."

"And that is exactly?" Isla asked her.

"Everything he never knew he desired," she said, toasting her friend with her glass before taking a long sip and praying all her dreams would come true.

. . .

WES GAMBLED THE REST OF THE BALL AND left it until the last dance before trying to find Miss Harlow York again to take her hand in another turn about the room.

He had promised her, after all, and they had an agreement. Before leaving the gentlemen to their games, he pocketed the few IOUs and blunt he had secured at Hazard and the faro table.

It did not take him long to locate Miss York. For the past several hours, his charge seemed to have gained a little popularity if the several gentlemen who stood about her and Viscountess Leigh were any indication.

Was one of the men present the very one she wished to impress? He slowly made his way toward her, speaking to several acquaintances as he went so as not to look too keen.

He was not. For all the pretty portrait she made for a man like himself to gaze upon, admire, and lust for, marriage was not a commitment he wanted to enter. Not yet at least. He was six and twenty, too young to want a wife.

But it did not change the fact flirting with the delightful, if not a little forward, Miss York did make attending the balls and parties just a tad bit more enjoyable.

He stood behind several gentlemen, meeting Miss York's eye above their heads, as they stood two or so inches shorter than himself. Her green eyes sparkled in humor and expectation, and he knew the reason why.

They shared a secret, and the little termagant knew he was about to ask her to dance.

"Miss York," he said, holding out his hand. "My dance, I believe."

She took his hand, and he walked her onto the ballroom floor. They joined other couples, the orchestra preparing to play the final song for the evening.

"I thought you may have forgotten me, my lord," she said, slipping into his arms. Wes ignored that she was a lovely height for a woman, not too short, making dancing uncomfortable, or a long meg who towered over him.

Again her breasts caught his attention, and his mouth watered at the thought of what delicate round buds awaited his tongue to lave and appreciate.

"I never go back on my word, Miss York." He pulled her into the dance and cast a glance to where she had been standing. Lord Abercromby, a viscount from Cumbria, had a nose almost as long as his name. Lord Hill was a more handsome fellow, although it was rumored he enjoyed a little rough play with his bedmates.

Wes frowned at the thought of Miss York being thrown about a bed before being made love to. No, Lord Hill would never do, and he would have to ensure her particular interest was not steering in that direction.

He turned them through the dance and studied the last of the gentlemen who stood watching them take a turn about the room. Lord Poulett. A gentleman of considerable wealth, even if the family had not been able to secure a title until the mid-1700s. They were new to the aristocracy, but that did not matter much, not when it was rumored he was worth over twenty thousand pounds per year.

"What do you think of my gentlemen admirers?" she asked, grinning at him like a little hellion.

He cleared his throat, trying to find the words that would not offend. "Well enough, I suppose, but I would stay clear of Lord Hill. He is not for you," he stated, not wanting to elaborate further.

"Oh, no, my lord. You cannot merely say that. You must tell me what you're hiding from my delicate female ears," she teased, blinking her eyelashes as if she were all naïve and had not been the one to come up with their ridiculous, if not genius, plan.

"Do you really wish to know?" he asked, fighting to keep the smirk from his lips.

"Of course. If I'm to consider Lord Hill, which I may or may not be, those particular details are mine and mine alone to know, but should I be, I would like to know any secrets that may make my decision have a better outcome."

"So Lord Hill is the gentleman you want as your husband?" he asked outright, his gut churning at the thought.

She shrugged one delicate shoulder, his attention snapping to the clear, perfect skin on her neck. "I'm not going to tell you that, my lord. You're merely here to help me gain the gentleman's attention. Nothing more."

"Well, if that is the case," he said, wanting Miss York to have nothing to do with Lord Hill. "Let me just warn you that unless you like a pink, stinging ass before lying with your husband each night, I would look elsewhere than his hand in marriage."

She gasped, her mouth agape, the teasing minx of a minute ago long gone. "What do you mean by such scandalous words, my lord?" she asked. "Are you saying he is violent to his bedmates?" She stared at Lord Hill, and he could see the disgust in her eyes.

Wes shook his head, leaning down to whisper in her ear, "He likes to spank his lovers, and if you're his wife, you will also receive those." He pulled back, fighting to keep the grin off his lips. "He does not do it to be cruel or to punish. Some women, and men included, enjoy such bed sport. You may find you do too. That is yet to be determined."

Miss York's face burned bright red, the tips of her ears even redder than her cheeks. "Do breathe, Miss York. I did not wish to shock you into a fainting spell."

Her mouth opened and closed several times before she managed, "Is that something that you enjoy, my lord?"

Wes grappled for words, having never been asked such a question in his life. And certainly not from a maid.

But how to answer it without scandalizing her more?

Four

"Miss York, that is a question with an answer that is not appropriate for your ears." Wes fought to keep his concentration on the dance and not on the inquisitive features of his partner.

"I beg to differ, my lord. And let us not forget that you started this conversation, or at least steered us down this inappropriate road, and now I shall not rest until I know. Do you or do you not like to be spanked?"

He ground his teeth, his cock twitching unhelpfully in his breeches. "I do not, no." But he would not mind slapping her fine ass for being so brash. Perhaps afterward he'd kiss it better ...

She sighed, moving her attention to something over his shoulder. "Well, that is too bad. For a moment, I thought you may be more mischievous than I knew."

"I'm mischievous enough, Miss York. I am helping you, am I not?"

"You are, and doing a fine job of it. Why, your interest in me has already garnered attention."

"And is one of the gentlemen from your admirers earlier about you? Are you willing to divulge to me yet whom you desire?"

She met his eyes, hers twinkling with enjoyment. His lips twitched at the sight of her relishing the evening and the caper they were taunting the *ton* with.

"You will not trick me into divulging my secret, my lord, but I promise you, in good time, you will know who it is that I admire and want. I shall not keep the secret hidden forever."

She watched him and the pit of his gut clenched. She was so pure and beautiful, but that paled in comparison to how much he was enjoying her company, her desire not to be as wellbred as she ought.

It made him wonder what else she would be willing to do to lure the man of her heart. "Your eyes are such a deep shade of green. I do not think I have ever seen anyone with the hue," Wes blurted, unsure where the words came from, only that he knew looking at her, he needed to state such a fact.

"You like my eyes then, my lord? Is that what you're trying to say?" she asked him.

"I suppose I am." He saw no reason why he

should lie. "I do not understand why you must play this game, Miss York. You're a beautiful woman. Your eyes are bright and wide, your nose is perfectly proportioned to your face, and you have pretty cheekbones when you smile. Not to mention your body is what men like me want to touch, and often. If this gentleman you admire so much has not shown interest until I have, mayhap he is not the man for you."

Pleasure flooded her features, and he hoped she did not read too much into his words. He was not in love with her. He liked her, most definitely, maybe even felt a little lust, but that was where it ended and would go no further.

"I understand what you're saying, but I think he merely needed a little push to see me this Season. How he has spoken about me and danced with me gives me more hope every hour." She grinned at him as he swung her to a stop as the dance ended. "You are the perfect man for me, my lord."

"To help you, you mean," he amended.

"To help me, of course," she agreed. He walked her back to Lady Leigh and spoke to Lord Leigh for several minutes before taking his leave. He strode from the room, other guests slowly making their way home now that the ball was over.

He stepped out onto the front steps of the Georgian home just as the breaking dawn kissed

London good morning. His helping Miss York was a good thing. He had never been asked to assist a young lady before, and if it meant Miss York gained the love of her heart, then it would make the Season less mundane and pointless as so many of them were.

HARLOW WALKED THROUGH HYDE PARK the following afternoon, her maid trailing behind her as she looked about for Lord Kemsley. She stopped under a large tree, shading her eyes as she studied who was taking the air this warm afternoon.

Disappointment stabbed at her. He was not here, but then she could understand why he would not be. She had not asked him to walk with her during her outings, but maybe she should. State it was another way of gaining her intended's interest in her.

"Miss York, good afternoon," Lord Hill stated, taking off his hat and bowing before her.

Harlow dipped into a curtsy, pasting on a smile that took more effort than it ought. "Lord Hill, how very good to see you again. Are you enjoying your walk?" she asked him, moving forward and noting he too followed at her side. The man was of similar height to Lord Kemsley, but where Kemsley was blond, Lord Hill was dark. And now, she couldn't help but see him spanking a woman's bottom every time she looked at him.

"I am, indeed. The day is warm, not a breath of wind, and I have come upon you. How could the day not improve with every tick of the clock when I'm in your presence?"

She smiled but ignored his words. "Are you attending the Bell's dinner this evening? I heard there are to be over fifty guests dining with Lord and Lady Bell prior to the ball."

"I am indeed," he repeated. "And from your words, I can assume that you, too, will be in attendance."

"That is right," she said. "I'm traveling with my sister Lady Billington and her husband, the viscount."

Lord Hill frowned at the mention of Billington, and she studied him, curious as to why the mention of her brother-in-law would cause offense or concern him. Maybe what Lord Kemsley said of Lord Hill was true, and he was not the kind of gentleman she ought to even pretend to have court her. She did not want to become involved in a scandal, not of her own making in any case.

"I look forward to seeing them again," he said, his words lacking the excitement upon their first meeting. "And may I be so bold as to secure the first two dances with you? If your hand is not already promised elsewhere."

Harlow could hardly say no to the gentleman when, in truth, she was not promised to anyone. Lord Kemsley had failed to secure her hand in the first two dances of tonight's ball, so she would not say no and be seen on the side of the ballroom floor during the two sets. What would Lord Hill think of her then?

"My hand is not promised to anyone, my lord. I shall save the first two dances if that is what you wish."

His eyes sparkled with expectation, and Harlow hoped he did not read into her agreement too much. "I hope it is what you want too, Miss York. I would not like to force you into anything you do not agree with."

His words left a sour taste in her mouth, but she shook her head, not wanting to be rude. "This is the Season, my lord. There are few whom I would not give the opportunity to dance with me. I wish to make my Season a success as much as anyone else," she said, hoping he would understand her answer and not read into her agreement as anything more than what she would do with anyone else.

She did not want him to believe himself special or a gentleman she wished would court her, for she did not. There was only one man for her, and she was determined to win Lord Kemsley's love before she returned to Grafton at the end of the Season.

That did not mean she would not use opportunities like the one that had just arisen before her, using Lord Hill to her advantage and allowing Lord Kemsley to believe she was interested in the gentleman.

"That is true, Miss York. Thank you for reminding me that we are all just searching for our perfect life matches."

She smiled, continuing on. Harlow searched her mind to think of something to discuss when a man appeared before them in the distance. He moved toward them with determined strides, and her mouth dried at the sight.

Lord Kemsley.

She fought back the sigh of relief and admiration that wanted to slip between her lips. He was so handsome and tall and caught the eye of anyone watching him.

Lord Hill mumbled something under his breath that she did not catch before she heard him bid her good afternoon.

Harlow managed to reply just as Lord Kemsley stopped before her, bowing in greeting. "Miss York, you looked as if you required saving," he said, looking in the direction Lord Hill had disappeared.

She slipped her arm about his, and they continued along the lawn. "I think you may be right with that summarization. Our conversation had come to a screeching, uncomfortable halt."

He chuckled and the deep, throaty sound made the pit of her stomach clench with warm heat. "An occupational hazard with Lord Hill, I'm afraid. He's not known for being stimulating, not in conversation or anything else."

Harlow raised her brow, studying his lordship. "And just what would anything else encompass, my lord? Is it something I should be aware of, or are you being purposefully vague?"

"Again, I'm being vague. I cannot allow such pretty ears to hear what I know of Lord Hill. But I will state yet again, do keep clear."

"You have already told me he likes to spank his lovers' bottoms. I fail to see what else he likes to do that is worse." She paused. "As for keeping my distance, if only I could," she sighed. "I have promised him the first two dances at this evening's ball after Lord and Lady Bell's dinner." She raised her brow at Kemsley. "Someone who is supposed to be helping me had not asked for my hand first, and I was forced to give myself to another." She pinned him with an accusatory stare, and he grinned.

"I will not allow you to give yourself to anyone unless you wish it, Miss York. Do you need me to dance with you instead? I can assume by your response to Lord Hill that he is not the gentleman you wish to acquire as your husband."

"Oh, heavens no, not at all. Lord Hill has

nothing on the man who makes my heart beat fast and my skin tingle."

"Tingle? Is it a nice tingle or an uncomfortable tingle? I must know."

Heat bloomed on her cheeks, and she shook her head. "Wouldn't you like to know, my lord," she said teasingly. "I will not answer such a question. It's not for you to know."

"But now I'm determined to find out," he answered, laughing. "One way or another, I shall tease it out of you, Miss York. I must know what sort of tingle it is you're feeling."

If only he would tease it out of her. Now that would be an enjoyable tingle, she was sure.

FIVE

The dinner at Lord and Lady Bell's Grosvenor Street home was a most sought-after invitation. Not to mention the ball afterward was rumored to be lively and always entertaining when Lady Bell hired entertainers who enjoyed the *demimonde* more so than the *beau monde*.

Harlow knew her invitation to the dinner was solely due to the fact she was a house guest of the Viscount and Viscountess Billington for the Season. Still ignoring all that, she walked into the dining room beside Lord Billington, determined to enjoy her evening among the *ton's* most influential families and friends.

A footman held out her chair, and she sat. Lord Hill sat across from her and bestowed a warm smile. She smiled in return and was thankful he was not beside her so she would not have to try to think of things to say to his lordship throughout dinner.

Beside her were Lord Abercromby and Lord Poulett, both men she had teased Lord Kemsley about regarding her dream spouse. Of course, neither of them were, but it was helpful that Lady Bell had seated her where she did.

Lord Kemsley strolled into the room, Dowager Randall on his arm, their heads bowed in quiet conversation. Harlow pushed down the jealousy that wanted to make her eyes narrow and her mouth pinch.

His lordship could speak to whomever he wanted. He was helping her and did not know it was him she desired at the conclusion of their lessons.

Even so, watching Lady Randall, a rich widow she had already come across in a private setting with Kemsley, was a hard reality to accept.

They sat several seats up from her on the opposite side, but close enough that she could hear Lord Kemsley's deep baritone.

"Are you enjoying the Season, Miss York?" Lord Abercromby asked her as the first course of turtle soup was placed before them.

"I am, Lord Abercromby. Now that my sister is happily settled, I feel much joy in what I have to look forward to."

"I, for one, am glad that you returned to town this Season. I did not think you would after your sister married the man I assumed you had feelings for," he said.

Harlow choked on her spoonful of soup and picked up her napkin, wiping her lips in an attempt to compose herself. She glanced down the table and found Lord Kemsley's gaze on her, his eyes taking in both her and Lord Abercromby.

"Not at all," she managed. "What the *ton* believed and what I feel are two different things. I do love Lord Billington, but as a brother-in-law, you understand," she stated, holding his eye until he nodded.

She continued to eat, refusing to look about and see if anyone else had noticed her faux pas. She hoped they had not.

"I'm glad to hear it. It gives gentlemen like me hope that your heart is not pining for a man you cannot have."

Harlow took a calming breath. Was the man daft? How could he even think she coveted her sister's husband? What was the *ton* thinking? Did they believe this at all? How mortifying.

"Do not be absurd," she blurted, needing to nip this rumor back into the ridiculous void it came from. "And I would be grateful that should you hear such scandalous rumors that you repeat my words to whoever is saying such things and correct their assumption."

He clasped his hand over his heart. "Of

course, Miss York. I will not disappoint you on your request."

"Good," she said. "See that you do not."

WES ONLY CAUGHT SMALL TIDBITS FROM Miss York's conversation with Lord Abercromby, but from her stony expression and thin, displeased lips, she was not enjoying her conversation with the viscount at all.

If only Lady Randall beside him would stop her unmasked suggestions on what they could enjoy after the ball, he could attempt to hear better of what Miss York spoke.

He ignored her ladyship as much as he could and was thankful when Lord FitzGeorge, to her left, pulled her into a conversation for several minutes so he could continue to eavesdrop on Miss York's conversation.

Why, he could not fathom. He was helping her, and he did get along with her well enough. He supposed that was sufficient reason, but maybe there was more to it than that.

She was devastatingly pretty. Each time he caught sight of her, talking, dancing, laughing ... a hunger growled within him, and wanted to claim her as his own.

But he was a rake, a rogue, a bachelor. Not looking for a bride, marriage, children, and commitments that would be lifelong. Not yet, at least.

The complexities of his thoughts of late must be because he agreed to help her, nothing more. They were friends, and he cared for her in that capacity. He ought not to read into his emotions any more than that.

He glanced at Harlow, and she was staring at the larks before her, the shriveled-up birds not to his liking either, and he waved his plate away.

She cringed, and she looked about the table, watching others devour the bite-sized birds, and her skin paled to a ghostly white.

"Miss York, are you well?" he asked, fearful she would be ill before the upper *ton*.

A footman came to her chair and helped her to stand. "If you will excuse me a moment," she said.

Without thinking, Wes followed her into the foyer, helping her toward the receiving room where they had congregated before dinner.

"A glass of lemonade," he called out to a footman, who ran off to do his bidding.

She sat on a settee, leaning her head in her hands as they waited. "Those little birds were the ugliest, most shriveled-up bits of bone and meat I have ever seen in my life. How could people place that in their mouths?" she asked him.

He chuckled, handing her the glass of lemonade delivered on a silver tray. "Most at the table probably dislike the bird as much as I and you do, Miss York, but eat it to be polite. I'm glad to see you are not such a sheep."

She sipped the lemonade, a little of her color coming back. "I'm glad I'm not the only one who refuses to accept such things so not to offend. I couldn't imagine biting on those tiny bones."

"Do not think about it," he said. "You may still cast up your accounts if you do."

She nodded, looking past him toward the door. "Should you be in here with me, Lord Kemsley? I know a footman is just outside, but we're relatively alone. You should return to the dinner."

"And if I do not want to?" he asked her, unsure where the words came from, but knowing they were the truth.

He did not want to go back and have to make pretty talk with the Lady Randall, whom he had no intention of fucking again, no matter how much she would like a tumble in his bed.

He would much rather help Miss York, the honest, sweet, in-love-with-someone-else, safe Miss York.

"I do not wish to compromise you, my lord. That would never help with my plan," she said, throwing him a small smile.

"Well, it would certainly be a different avenue to tread than the one you had so carefully planned." Wes leaned back on the settee, ensuring she sipped the remainder of her lemonade. "We could discuss other ways to gain the interest of the man you wish to marry if you like. By the time we return, the larks will be gone."

"I would like that very much," she said, turning to face him more. "Tell me what else I can do to gain the attention of the man I adore. I need to know all the lures there are to help me."

Wes glanced over his shoulder, ensuring the door remained open, but they were alone. "I think we should practice the skills of seduction, but skills that have nothing to do with touching, nothing tactile."

She frowned at him. "I'm not sure I understand your meaning, my lord," she said.

Wes crossed his legs, making himself comfortable. "A look across a ballroom between two people can be more impactful than a dance or even a kiss. So much can be said, can be revealed within another person's eyes. The way a man or woman may stare at each other with such intensity that you know what the other person is thinking without a word spoken. A person's looks can also twist a gaze into being so much more. So much so that deep within your soul, the pit of your stomach may clench, tumble about, and make your breath catch."

"Gosh, I had no idea," she breathed, biting her lip.

Wes swallowed, schooling his features so as

not to succumb to his own words and start seeing looks and stares from Miss York that were not for him.

"Try it on me, Miss York. Look at me as if I'm the only man you want in the world. The only man you want in your bed."

She licked her lips, nodding in agreement before she met his gaze. Her eyes dipped to his lips before meeting his. The want and need, the pleading he read in her green depths, made his heart thump hard in his chest.

The breath in his lungs seized, and he fought not to fall under her spell. She was already very good at gifting a look that made him believe he was the man she wanted. The only man for her.

Her mouth opened on a soft sigh before she gave him a small smile and looked back at her hands.

Wes sat there for several beats of his heart, unsure of what had just occurred. His body felt all at sea, rocking about with the intensity, the honesty behind her gaze.

"You are very good already at that, Miss York," he said. "You should look at your gentleman more that way, and I believe he would be malleable in your hands."

She nodded. "Did you believe how I looked at you, my lord?" She paused. "I mean, I know we are but friends, but if we were not, would a look I just bestowed upon you make you want to pursue me? Would it make you want to come and talk to me, whisk me away for a secret kiss?"

God damn it all to hell. This was not where he thought this little lesson would lead. Not because kissing Miss York would not be entertaining and most likely pleasurable, but because he never told anyone before in his life the reaction he had to them. But then, he had never felt before for a woman what he was feeling right now in the receiving room of Lord and Lady Bell's house.

"If a woman looked at me the way you have mastered, I would do more than whisk her away to a secluded part of the ball, Miss York. She would be in my arms and well-kissed before she could blink."

"Truly?" she asked, amazement in her tone. "I have never kissed a man before, but to think I would raise such wants and needs in another is a promising sign. Your lessons must be working, my lord."

Wes raised one brow. "Possibly too well," he quipped.

"Here you are," Lady Bell said, sighing in relief. "I do apologize for the larks. I know they're not the prettiest plate," she said, sitting beside Miss York and taking the empty glass of lemonade. "You look like your color is back, and I believe the footman has been present the whole time you've been in here, so I will not chastise you very much, Lord Kemsley, but please do not be alone again with Miss York again. That is not allowed under my roof, you understand."

"I apologize, my lady. We are friends, and I wished to check on Miss York, nothing more. There was staff around, as you said, not just chaperoning this room but moving about for the ball to be held soon."

"Yes, which will be here before we know it, so do follow me and return to the dining room. There are several courses left. I promise those are much more appealing than the larks."

Wes helped Miss York to stand, and his hand brushed the underside of her arm above her elbow where her silk glove failed to cover. He closed his eyes and fought the urge to stroke her soft skin, to bathe in her nearness. She was meant for someone else. Was in love with another. He could not seduce her for his selfish means, only to leave her when he would not marry. Not because he did not like her very much, but merely because he enjoyed being a rogue, a bachelor. His younger brother living in Wales was married and with a son. In all truth, there was no reason at all he needed to wed just to beget an heir. He glanced down at Miss York and caught her watching him, her eyes beckoning him for things he could not give her.

Perhaps these lessons had been a bad idea after all.

Six

Harlow returned to the table, escorted by Lady Bell, and was happy to see the larks had been replaced as promised with roast lamb, boiled bacon cheek, and vegetables. Lord Kemsley returned to his seat, talking softly with Lady Randall, who looked more than pleased that he was back at her side again.

She spoke to Lord Poulett about the weather and the upcoming ball, but her heart was not engaged enough to keep the conversation going any longer than it already had. All she could think about, all her body remembered, was the last lesson she had shared with Lord Kemsley.

Could a look between two people really alter one's evening or even their future? He stated she had mastered the gaze very well, understood what he was suggesting she do to her pretend intended, and it certainly seemed to spark something with his lordship. The fire that had ignited in his eyes told her that was true.

Had her glances made fire lick at his soul as it had hers? She finished the small portion of lamb and watched Lord Kemsley from her position at the table.

He picked up his glass of wine, his hands large and covering most of the crystal, and nerves pooled in her stomach. What would it feel like to have those hands on her? They were strong and looked unpampered, unlike so many other men in the *ton*. Did he do manual labor she did not know about? What was that work if he did? Images of him laboring horses at the mews, his muscular body free from the restraints of gentleman's attire, sweating in the midday sun flooded her mind. Or perhaps he helped cut the wood for the fires ... his strong arms swinging an axe down on wood, the muscles flexing with every stroke.

He sipped from his glass, and their eyes met. A delicious feeling fluttered inside her stomach, and not for anything could she look away.

Instead, Harlow dipped her attention to where his lips kissed the crystal, and farther still. His strong chest and broad shoulders, the perfectly tied cravat that sat about his neck, she couldn't help but wonder what it smelled like.

No, she did know the answer to her thought. Lord Kemsley would smell lovely, possibly like sandalwood or some other earthy tone she had always admired. He continued to stare at her, and she shifted on her chair, achingly aware of how he made her feel. As if her body was not her own and he could make her do whatever he wished.

She wasn't unsure that he could not.

The muffled voice of Lady Fairchild floated to her, and the mention of Kemsley's name caught her attention. "Lord Kemsley is very handsome, is he not?" her ladyship said to Lady Bell to her right, pulling their host's attention away from her dinner.

Heat kissed Harlow's cheeks, and she took a long sip of her wine. "He is not difficult to look at," she agreed. "A very accommodating gentleman, I think. What a shame he is determined to be a bachelor forever."

Lady Fairchild chuckled, sighing as her attention slipped to Kemsley, who sat back while the footman placed down the next course. "These determined bachelors keep everyone on their toes and give us plenty of entertainment throughout the Season, but anything more than that, and I fear hearts are destined for heartache."

Had Lady Fairchild noticed Kemsley leave with her and thought her friendship with his lordship was doomed to end with her brokenhearted? She hoped that was not the case, but then he had said himself he did not want to marry. A warning, even if not directed at her, one she ought to heed.

"It is lucky for those seeking a match that there are others more than willing to fill that void, is it not?" Lady Bell said, her attempt to stop talking about Lord Kemsley seemingly working. Lady Fairchild was a renowned gossip, after all.

"It is indeed," Lady Fairchild stated. "Perhaps we ought to tell the Lady Randall such truths, so she does not make a fool of herself at the table."

Relief poured through her that they were not talking of her but of Lady Randall, quickly followed by despair. Harlow glanced at the Lady Randall, now giggling uncontrollably next to Kemsley, her gloved hand firmly about his upper arm. Even from here, Harlow could see she was doing more than a passing touch, had instead gripped his upper arm, her fingers working his muscle in an embrace not fit for a dinner table.

The woman was far too forward when in company.

Lady Bell cleared her throat, casting the dowager Randall a warning stare. The widow seemed to heed the direction and sat back in her chair, the serene, perfect widow once more.

"He will never marry her, you know. He likes the chase and nothing more. As much as I like Lord Kemsley, he's the king of all rogues, and any woman seeking his heart will be marked for disappointment," Lady Fairchild stated bluntly.

Harlow watched Lady Bell school her features, and she could not help but wonder if the Lady Randall herself had once hoped for a future with the earl that had not materialized.

Thank heavens she had only told Isla of her plans, and no one knew what her hopes were for the future. But was Lady Fairchild correct? Was she hoping for a future, a miracle with Kemsley that would not materialize?

He enjoyed the company of women, even her company. His lessons were helpful, but were they making any difference in how she made him think about her?

She couldn't help but think, at this point, they had not.

LATER THAT EVENING, HARLOW DANCED the first two dances with Lord Hill as promised. Sweat ran down his lordship's face profusely, and several times he had to stop and wipe his forehead with his handkerchief. The dances seemed never-ending, and she was relieved when they finally finished.

Harlow lifted her hand to her nose, fighting the stench of his lordship while he walked her back to Lady Leigh. The cloying scent of his unwashed skin wafted through the air, and she hoped those who danced about and with them did not think it was she who had not pre-prepared herself for the evening's entertainment.

After several minutes of benign conversation, Harlow excused herself, dipping into a curtsy before starting for the terrace doors. She needed air. The odor clung to her nostrils, and not another moment of the ball could be enjoyed.

Stepping out onto the large flagstone terrace, she was glad to see others mingling outside, enjoying refreshments and idle chatter among friends.

Harlow walked to the railing and glanced out over the darkened gardens. She took a deep breath and started when a warm, large hand slipped against her back. A tall, welcome gentleman brushed past her before idly leaning against the stone railing, grinning at her.

"Was your dance not to your liking, Miss York? You raced out of the ballroom as if the devil himself was nipping at your silk slippers."

"A moment's peace and fresh air is all I require," she said, taking her own advice and breathing deep, removing the vile stench still attached to her nostrils.

Lord Hill needed to learn proper hygiene.

"Do you wish to be alone?" he asked, moving away from her a little.

Without thought, Harlow reached for his hand, pulling him near. "No," she said, quickly releasing him. She looked about them, glad no one was paying them any heed, and saw what she had just done. "I would welcome your company. Perhaps you could give me another lesson?"

"Another?" He grinned, watching her keenly. "I'm afraid our lessons do have a limit to what I can teach you." He licked his lips, and fire coursed through her blood.

"We have spoken of dancing, touching, and how one ought to look at the person they wish to seduce to their side, but I think we shall have to double down on these points instead of learning anything else."

Disappointment stabbed at Harlow, and she frowned. Not wanting that at all. She wanted to spend as much time with his lordship as she could and learn all she could to win his heart.

To seduce him to her side.

"But I need to know all that there is. Why can you not teach me more? Surely there are other things we can do," she begged him.

A muscle worked in his jaw, and he scuffed his Hessian boots on the terrace. "Of course there is, but those lessons are not without risk. I will not ruin your reputation."

She scoffed, shaking her head. "Lord Kemsley, surely what else you know is not going to be as bad as all that," she stated, a little part of her hoping she was wrong. What he knew would be wicked and wild, everything she wanted to be when it came to him.

His throat worked on a swallow. "Not that I

should be telling you this, Miss York, but when I wish to seduce a woman, I may whisk her to a private part of the house hosting a ball or dinner. I may walk with her on the terrace and disappear into the darkened gardens."

Harlow felt her eyes grow wide and hope bloom in her soul. "What would you do with your lady then, my lord? Please tell me. I must know all," she said, a little part of her hoping that he would whisk her into the gardens and kiss her until breaking dawn.

"Well," he said, leaning close to ensure privacy. "I may talk to the woman, mention how beautiful she looked in her gown. I may even attempt to touch her somehow, play with a lock of hair that had fallen from its pins, or touch her arm or hand, hoping she would wish for more of me before we parted."

His voice dipped to a deep baritone, coaxing, and nothing like she had heard from him before. It was as if he were thinking of her being his next paramour.

How she wished he were.

"And then you would steal a kiss?" she asked, holding his gaze.

He nodded, his attention dipping to her lips. Harlow bit hers and thought of how to use what his lordship taught her against him. She had to know, had to have him push past this barrier he had placed on their lessons and know all there was. If she could kiss him, surely that would lead to affection.

Lead to him giving up his bachelorhood, his rakish life, and becoming her husband.

His lips twitched, and he shrugged. "Perhaps a kiss or perhaps something else just as wicked," he quipped, wiggling his brows.

Harlow gaped at the possibilities of something else just as wicked. Her heart pumped loudly in her chest, and her determination to get what she wanted overrode all her common sense and decorum.

"I want you to teach me how to kiss a man. If I know this, I'm certain I can persuade the man I want to marry that I am his perfect match in every single way."

It was Lord Kemsley's turn to gape, and he stared at her for several moments before looking about them to ensure privacy. "I will not kiss you, Harlow. That is not in our agreement."

Harlow fought the urge to stomp her foot. "We are friends and nothing more. What is the harm in you teaching me such a thing? I will not bite you, but I would hate to make such a mistake with the man I wish to marry should I not know what I'm doing. Please, my lord. Do not let me down when I'm close to getting what I want."

You ...

SEVEN

Wes fought the urge to agree to everything Harlow York asked of him. He could not steal her away and give her kissing lessons, no matter how tempting that thought was.

She was a delectable little doll, and should she have been a widow or even a disgruntled wife in society, he knew he would have long tried to tumble her onto a bed and fuck the night away with her, with no guilt whatsoever.

But she was not. She was an innocent maid, practically still a debutante since this was her second Season. Not to mention she was under scrutiny more than most due to being the Season's diamond last year.

He could not kiss her.

He could not.

He closed his eyes, fighting the rogue that roared within him to do all that he should not.

Steal her away around the terrace corner, run her behind an oversized hedge and take those wicked lips that pouted up at him right at this moment.

Damn it all to hell, she was good at getting what she wanted, or at least when it came to trying to persuade him to break all his rules with innocent misses.

"I cannot give you such lessons, Harlow. You know I cannot. If we're caught, you marry a man you do not want, and I lose the freedom I so adore. Our marriage would be hell, and I shall not have you suffer the consequences of such a mistake. It is not fair."

"But we will not be caught," she pleaded. "We shall be careful."

Wes shook his head. "No, I will not be persuaded."

Her mouth tightened into an irritated pucker before she turned on her heel and left him alone on the terrace. He watched her return to the ball, part of him disappointed he had not sampled her inviting mouth, but he was not for her.

He could not cross that line, no matter how much he may long to. She was a maid. To kiss him could lead to scandal and ruination, and that was not what their lessons were about. He was to help her, not hinder her road toward a happy ever after with whomever it was she wanted at her side for the rest of her life.

With no one else on the terrace with whom

he wished to converse, he returned to the ball and watched from the safety of the wall and several matrons who stood in front of him as Miss York was asked to dance with Lord Poulett.

The gentleman's eyes burned with interest in Miss York, and he ground his teeth. Was this the gentleman whom she wanted to marry? She certainly looked more than pleased, smiling up at the man as if he were the stars and moon in her small, innocent universe.

Lord Poulett pulled her into his arms as they started to dance. Wes took a calming breath, resolving himself to remain strong. She would not coax him into being his rogue self.

Not with her in any case.

She was the sister-in-law of one of his good friends. To take the lessons past the line of propriety would risk that friendship, among others. He would not do it.

Not willing to watch another moment of her wide smiles up at Lord Poulett, he started for the door. Whites would be more enjoyable in any case and safer for her reputation, which was skating on thin ice, especially when she begged him to do wicked things.

He was a man after all. His resolve only went so far.

. . .

WES AVOIDED MISS YORK FOR TWO DAYS before his attendance at the Daniels' masked ball. It was an evening he never missed. Since arriving in town at eighteen, he had attended Lord and Lady Daniels' annual mask and would not allow Miss York and her allure to stop him.

Not that she would be here this evening. This ball, hosted by the upper echelon of society, was not for the faint of heart. There were normally only married couples, widows and widowers, and sometimes even those from the *demimonde* who attended. Debutantes were not allowed, and so this evening he ought to be free to enjoy himself and not be tempted into a situation that could lead them both astray from where their lives wished to go.

Wes smiled as he spied his mother talking to Lady Daniels, and he joined her, bussing her cheek in welcome. "Mama, Lady Daniels, it is good to see you both. I hope you have room on your card for a turn about the dance floor with me, Mama?" he asked, smiling when she laughed like a young woman new to town.

"Wes, my darling boy. I had hoped to see you here. You really ought to move home and not board at the Albany. I enjoy my time here in town more when I can live vicariously through you."

He chuckled, taking a glass of brandy from a passing footman and sipping slowly. "I do not think you wish any such thing," he teased. "More likely, you wish to persuade me toward some marriageable miss you have chosen for me."

His mother slapped his arm with her fan while Lady Daniels chuckled behind her gloved fingers. "Lord Kemsley, you are a devil, but that is why we enjoy you so much. You are never boring. I shall give you that," Lady Daniels said before excusing herself to join another party of friends.

His mama studied him for a moment, a wistful smile on her face. "Your brother is happy, I only want the same for you." She paused, gesturing to her face. "Do you like my mask? I had it made especially by the modiste to match my gown."

"It suits you very well," he said, just as the room filled with murmured gasps and chatter.

He glanced toward the ballroom doors, and his heart stopped at the sight of the woman who stood there. He narrowed his eyes, trying to recognize the woman, his body alight with fire at the exotic, mysteriousness of her.

"I see Lord and Lady Billington have arrived, but I'm surprised they have brought Miss York. She is not married, as you know."

Wes choked on his brandy. That was Harlow?

Under the emerald-colored domino, a shimmering gold empire-cut gown accentuated a lithe, desirable body he had admired long before their little game of instruction began.

Miss York pushed the domino's hood away from her hair, revealing long, brown locks curled about her shoulders instead of up as they usually were. A black silk mask sat across her eyes and nose, her lips painted in a deep rouge. Wes swallowed. Hard.

She was even more kissable now.

However would he not relent and give her what she wanted? Instruction on how to use those lips to her advantage.

He narrowed his eyes, thinking of the man who would eventually get to taste her, touch her, and he fisted his hands at his sides, his body a temple of controlled annoyance.

"She's a lovely girl and good friends with Lady Leigh, I hear," his mama said, watching him keenly before she turned her attention back to Miss York, who was now making her way through the throng of guests. "You ought to ask her to dance, Wes. I think she would like that very much," his mother said, a teasing light in her eyes.

He ignored her look and cleared his throat. "I will dance with her and many others, Mother. I would not be a gentleman if I did not do my duty."

His mother scoffed. "A sister to a viscountess and best friends with another, why she will make some gentleman a suitable bride."

Wes bowed, the need to take his leave riding hard on his coattails. "If you'll excuse me. I see a friend I wish to speak to." He moved away from his mother before she dragged him over to Miss York and demand he marry her at once.

He would seek out Miss York later. He did not want his mama to think he was keen on the chit or be one of the first gentlemen at her side. They were friends, yes, but nothing more than that. Miss York needed time for the man she did wish to marry to come to greet her and improve on their acquaintance.

He moved to where Lord and Lady Daniels had placed large, potted shrubbery in the ballroom for decoration and watched as Miss York was soon surrounded by a gaggle of gentlemen admirers. Just as it should be.

Lord Hill was among them yet again. The man would need to be deterred from carrying on his courtship of Harlow. He was not right for her. She deserved someone who would at least attempt to have a happy marriage, and Miss York would not be granted one with his lordship.

Why do you care? a warning voice interjected in his mind.

He pushed the unhelpful thought aside. He wasn't so much of a rogue that he did not care for women at all. And Harlow was his friend.

She took Lord Abercromby's hand, and he led her out onto the floor for a country dance. For several minutes Wes watched her move up and down the ballroom floor. Her enthusiastic laughter made his lips twitch, and he could not help but admire her natural beauty, her *joie de vivre* she always sported.

His body thrummed with the need to be near her, to speak to her, to continue their lessons.

You want to do more than verbally instruct her.

That damn voice was back again, and he inwardly swore. He did not want to ruin her, but he could not ignore what his body was telling him. He did desire her. He did want to kiss her.

And mayhap not merely because she needed to learn how to seduce the man she wished to marry.

He ground his teeth. Who was that man in any case? Was it Lord Abercromby who now turned her about the floor? He was certainly suitable, and she seemed to enjoy his company more than anyone else he had seen. Large, overbearing nose notwithstanding.

Was he the man she wanted to steal away and kiss, seduce into marrying her?

A footman passed, and he stole two glasses of brandy, downing one immediately before striding out of the ballroom. He could not watch another moment. Not when his mind was playing tricks on him, making him think jealous things he ought not to be.

She was his friend. She was his student.

She was not, and never would be, his lover.

EIGHT

Harlow knew the exact moment that Lord Kemsley had slipped from the ballroom. It was as if her body was attuned to his every location, his mood, his looks, his every word.

But he was not here now, even though he had just been watching her dance, the annoyance written across his visage enough to give her a modicum of hope that he was feeling something for her.

What that something was, she could not say, but she was determined to find out.

After the dance, she bade Lord Abercromby a good evening and left the ballroom. She did not know where Lord Kemsley had gone, but until she found him, she would pretend to be looking for the retiring room should anyone come across her.

The house was large, with several passages

leading off from the ballroom, which was on the ground floor. She heard several ladies start up the stairs and knew the retiring room must be on the first floor. Forgoing the company of others, she walked along a darkened passage. Several rooms were closed off in this hallway, and she skidded to a stop when she came to the billiards room and Lord Kemsley leaning over the table, hitting a little green ball with more ire and determination than she thought his singular game involving one required.

She leaned up against the doorframe and crossed her arms over her chest. "Is it time for my lesson? Since you left the ballroom, I thought I would come here and find you instead."

His strike against the ball made a loud clicking sound, and he stood, leaning against his billiard stick. "You should not have followed me, Miss York. We have discussed what should happen should you be caught with me."

"I know we have," she said, entering the room and closing the door behind her. "But we will not be. No one is taking any notice of me, and you left long before I did. You worry too much that people will think something is happening between us when it is not." Harlow watched Kemsley, hoping her words may spark some kind of denial, but disappointingly he nodded in agreement.

"Good, that is how it ought to be," he said.

But is that how we want it to be? She wanted to ask him. Instead, she sauntered into the room as seductively as she knew how and leaned against the billiards table instead.

"I still think you should teach me how to kiss. What if my intended steals a kiss to see if I'm passionate enough for him to be his wife, and I fumble the whole thing? I shall have you to blame, you know, and that will never do."

His gaze dipped to her lips. Tonight she had been bold and had begged Lila to allow her to rub a little rouge on her lips since they were all wearing masks, and she had thankfully agreed.

The darkening hunger in Kemsley's eyes told her that mayhap her attempt to appear alluring, a siren instead of an innocent debutante, may have paid off.

Or very well would soon.

He took his billiard stick and placed it back in a wooden holder where others sat before running a hand through his hair. "You're being difficult, Miss York."

"I'm not," she argued. "We are friends, and there is nothing untoward happening between us, nor will it even if you instruct me in this new lesson. You're scared, that's what you are. I did not think rogues were ever intimidated about kissing a woman."

He looked at her as if she had lost part of her

mind, which she would certainly do if he did not kiss her and soon.

The maddening man.

"I'm not scared of kissing you. I merely do not want you to think more of the kiss than you ought." A muscle worked in his jaw as he watched her. "Kisses sometimes become passionate, no matter how they start, and I do not want you to commence thinking of me in a different light than you do now."

Unlikely. She already thought of him as the brightest light in her life, and there would be no changing that. But his words gave her hope that he would change her mind and teach her to kiss.

Her stomach fluttered at the thought, and she chose her next words carefully.

"I will not change my mind about you, Lord Kemsley. I know very well your lifestyle and that you wish to keep it. I also do not look at you in that romantic way. I like another. We have been through this. I promise you, your virtue is safe with me," she finished, glad her words came out matter-of-fact and to the point.

Even if they were a whole lot of bollocks.

He hesitated for just a moment before she knew she had won this small but also momentous battle. "Very well. Sit on the settee, and we shall begin. I shall explain what you should do, and we will practice."

Harlow did as he asked, swallowing her

squeal of excitement. Tonight, right this moment, she was going to have her first kiss. She sat and settled the domino and her gown about her, facing his lordship, who joined her.

He leaned close. "When a couple kiss, certain things may occur before the actual event."

She nodded, hoping her eyes were not wide and in awe of him. They certainly felt as wide as saucers right at this moment. "I understand. Like the looks we have already gone over, you mean," she stated.

"That is correct." His hand slipped onto her shoulder, one finger moving slowly over the bare skin on her neck to tilt up her chin. "A gentleman may also touch you a little, move his fingers over your skin, revel in the feel of you."

"Yes," she gasped, clearing her throat, hoping he could not hear her heart pumping loudly in her chest. "Does my skin feel soft enough to you?" She needed to know, required him to touch more of her.

Kiss me already.

"It is soft." He dipped his head to the curve of her neck. "You smell divine, like roses."

Harlow fought the urge to grin at his words and schooled her features into that of a compliant student willing to learn. "Do you think my intended will say such things?"

Lord Kemsley pulled back and met her eyes,

and she wondered what was going through his beautiful brain.

He nodded. "Hmm, yes, of course. Now on with the lesson."

MISS YORK'S WORDS PULLED WES BACK from the precipice of forgetting what exactly he was doing right at this moment with her. He was not supposed to be enjoying having her in his arms.

Not so much in any case.

Of course, he knew that he would, but not to the point that he would forget that he was teaching, instructing her on the art of seduction for her intended and forgetting during that instruction that he was a player in her game, not a participant she wished to seduce.

"A man may kiss his way up your neck, nibble on the lobe of your ear. Like this," he said, biting the flesh between his teeth and teasing it with his tongue.

He felt her shiver in his arms, and her hands came up to rest on his shoulders, her fingers digging into him through his coat.

"Do not be alarmed if this occurs. Do not pull away. Merely revel in the feel of your lover and how he makes *you* feel."

"I understand," she barely mumbled, her voice low and quiet. He glanced at her as he kissed the underside of her ear. Her eyes were closed, her mouth slightly parted.

Damn, she was a beauty, so reactive and perfect. The gentleman, whomever that was she had set her cap on, was a lucky man indeed.

"He may then pull back just enough to come before you." Wes took in her features, her long, dark eyelashes that swept closed over her pinkened cheeks. Her lips were pouty and lush, perfect for kissing.

"Open your eyes, Harlow, and look at me."

She did as he bade, watching him without a whisper of a word.

"You may look at each other like this. A final pause before you would kiss. If you wanted to stop progressing further, this is where you would pull away."

Her attention dipped to his mouth, and he hoped she could not feel the beat of his heart through his evening wear. He had not expected to react so strongly toward her, even pretending and teaching as he was.

To want her as much as he did.

Not forever, but certainly for right now.

"What happens next?" she asked, licking her lips and sending a bolt of desire to his cock.

"I would start by kissing you, slowly at first, little brushes of our lips to entice you to copy me, do as I am."

His body burned with expectation and need.

He bridged the space separating them, and their lips touched.

He closed his eyes with a sigh. Her lips were as soft as he thought, full and seeking just as he hoped. He brushed against her, taunting her, pursuing a response, and he was not disappointed.

Her hands came up to clasp the base of his neck, her fingers spiking into his hair before her lips pressed harder against his mouth. "Now, you must open for me, kiss me as if you cannot get enough of me. As if the taste and feel of me will never be enough. That your life itself will be over should you not throw yourself into my arms."

She nodded and closed the space between them. Her mouth opened, and Wes did the same, seeking her tongue with his, moving to deepen the embrace and taste her as he had longed to do. He could not stop tasting her.

She pulled back, her eyes wide. "Your tongue, what was it that you just did?" she asked him.

"You may do the same to me. Just follow my lead." He was most certainly going to hell for making an innocent woman demean herself so much with him. A man who would never be her husband.

But nor could he help himself. He wanted her to kiss him.

Now.

She closed the space between them, her hands

clasping his jaw as her lips touched his for a third time. Fire coursed in his blood and exploded into a wildfire when her tongue tentatively dipped into his mouth.

He kissed her back and held nothing from her. He took her mouth in a searing kiss that made him dizzy with need. Their tongues tangled, her little mews of surprise, of enjoyment, heightening his need to an uncontrollable pitch.

Without thinking, he wrenched her close, her breasts pushing hard against his chest. He fought to keep his hands on her hips, to not slip higher on her person and clutch at her abundant breasts.

The kiss continued, their mouths fused, tongues tangling, taking, fighting for dominion. It was too much, and yet not enough. Something told him that it would never be enough. Not when it came to Harlow York.

Wes wrenched from her hold, his breathing ragged. "I think that should conclude our lesson," he said, placing much-needed space between them. "This brings the kissing portion of my instruction to a close, and you passed with flying colors." He knew his words sounded absurd and out of place after what they had just done. Not to mention far too high-pitched.

She had passed his kissing test?

He was sure that he had failed it.

Miserably.

NINE

The following morning Harlow slept late, lying on her soft bed and remembering all that had happened the night before with Lord Kemsley. What a marvelous gift his kissing instruction had been. Not to mention she couldn't help but think that he had lost a little of his control when she had been in his arms.

Harlow flopped on her back, staring at the ornate ceiling at her sister's home with the viscount. Soon, if all her plans came to fruition, she too would have a house just like this one, but with Kemsley.

She had never been to his London home, but she was curious about what it may look like. He rented an Albany apartment, but his mother had opened their house on Hanover Square for the Season.

Not far from where she now stayed. With her

maid in tow, she could happen to stroll past and see what may possibly be hers one day.

If she could make him fall in love with her. Make herself indispensable to his lordship.

A knock sounded on her door, and without waiting for an answer, her sister entered, carrying Harlow's walking gown. "Good morning, dearest, or should I say afternoon since you're being utterly a lump and sleeping all day."

Harlow chuckled, sitting up, watching as her sister hung her gown in the armoire. "What are you doing with my dress? Have you chosen a different occupation in this house other than the lady of the manor?" Harlow asked, smiling at her witticism.

Lila rolled her eyes and came and sat on the end of the bed. "I came across your maid, and she looked a little busy with her chores, and I offered to bring up your gown. I was coming to see you in any case."

"You were?" Harlow asked. "What brings you to my room?"

"Well, as for that," her sister stated, watching her. "Have you forgotten we're to promenade in the park today in the carriage? I assume Lord Kemsley will be there, and you seem to be spending a great deal of time with his lordship. No matter what is said about him, he certainly seems to be courting you," Lila said.

Harlow would not let her sister's words give

her hope. "Of course, I remember we're to promenade," she said, smoothing her bedding over her legs. "Lord Kemsley is a family friend, one of your husband's if I need remind you. He is merely being kind to me, nothing more. Please do not make sly remarks about courtship around him. I do not want to make him uncomfortable should we see him." To have her sister acting as the matchmaker and giving Lord Kemsley the idea that she liked him and not the imaginary man she had persuaded him to think was real would be disastrous. He would not help her if he thought such a thing, and she needed him to spend time with her. Get to know her enough that he fell in love.

"I will not interfere, I promise. But I did notice that you already spend a great deal of time together at the balls, and he came to your aid at the dinner when the larks made you unwell. Maybe he likes you, Harlow?"

She shrugged. "I do not know what he feels, but my emotions and thoughts are unchanged. I want him to be my husband. I cannot think of anyone but his lordship who would suit me. We have wonderful conversations, he makes me laugh, and he's a kind gentleman, no matter if he has been a rake in the past. But he must not know my feelings are engaged. He's a rake after all, and easily frightened off."

Her sister grinned, shaking her head. "Well,

whatever you're doing to engage his lordship certainly seems to be working, and I would say to you to continue, but do not overstep the bounds of propriety."

Harlow scoffed, throwing her sister a dubious look. "Lila, really. You cannot say such a thing to me when you did not obey that rule yourself last year. Should I remind you what you told me happened between yourself and Lord Billington?"

Her sister's cheeks turned a rosy pink, and she stood, striding to the door. "No need, sister. I understand you perfectly well, but I do not want to see you hurt. Guard your heart and reputation until you are certain of him. That is all the advice I'm going to mete you." Lila gestured to the gown she had just hung in the wardrobe. "Now dress. We leave in an hour for the park."

INSTEAD OF DRESSING IN HER MORNING gown, Harlow decided a ride in the park would be much more preferable than the carriage. She changed into her dark-blue riding gown and sent her maid to have one of the mares saddled posthaste.

Upon meeting her sister in the foyer, although Lila was disappointed she would not be riding with them in the carriage, being a lover of horses herself she could understand Harlow wished to ride instead.

"I shall walk near you, but on my mount. We can still speak," she said, just as a footman notified them all that the carriage was ready and her horse also.

It did not take them long to reach the park. A cooling breeze fluttered the feathers on her hat, and she walked her mount behind the carriage and halted whenever her sister stopped to converse with other members of the *ton*.

Harlow took in who was present, nodding in acknowledgment to Lord Abercromby and Lord FitzGeorge, who stood under a large oak with two young ladies.

A family with several children, ranging from infancy to adolescence, picnicked by the Serpentine, the elder children playing and chasing each other about.

Her horse stomped its hoof, shaking its head as she waited for her sister's carriage to move forward. Just when her sister bid good afternoon to Lord and Lady Davies, one of the children by the lake hit a hard ball with a bat that set off a loud crack.

Her mare shied to the side, and Harlow let out a yelp, clutching at the reins. She thought she had settled her mount before another crack sounded, and there was no stopping her horse this time.

The mare reared and then bolted across the park. For a moment, Harlow could do nothing but hold on. The thought of jumping off flittered through her mind, but then she decided against it when the ground rushed past her feet at break-neck speed.

She sat low in her saddle, pulling with all her might to slow her horse, but with little success. Her mare was scared, bolting without thought or caution.

Her heart beat loud in her ears, her arms shaking as she struggled to pull her mount up, to bring it to a halt. Thundering hooves sounded behind her, but she dared not look. Like a knight in shining armor, a horse and man came along her side, a hand reaching out to clasp her horse's bridle.

Only then did Harlow glance to see who had come to her rescue.

"Woo, mare," he cooed to her horse, pulling up both horses, his arms straining with the effort. "Woo now," he said again, and finally, Harlow felt her horse slow.

When they were stationary once more, only then did she dare speak. "Lord Kemsley, how will I ever thank you?" she gasped, her body shaking with fear and weariness.

Without a word, he jumped from his horse and pulled her from her mount before wrenching her into his arms, his hold absolute.

"I saw your horse bolt and thought the worst would happen to you."

Warmth flowed through her limbs, stopping them from feeling like they would collapse under her. His sweet and heartfelt words made her want to do more than hug him back.

"I am well. No harm has come to me. Thanks to you," she said, her voice still shaky. She looked up and met his eyes. His fear burned in his blue gaze, and her heart did a little flip. She had not expected him to have such a profound reaction to her dilemma, but seeing him, hearing his words, and what he had done to save her made hope alight in her heart.

And would not let go.

WES HAD COME DOWN TO THE PARK TO enjoy a quiet ride along Rotten Row; he had not expected to see a horse bolting across Hyde Park as if a whip had been slapped across its hide several times.

The fear that lodged in his throat when he realized the woman trying to pull up the mount was Harlow had sent a cold shiver of dread down his spine that still would not dissipate, even with her in his arms.

He stared at her, checking that she was well and no harm had come to her before the sounds of Lady Billington shouting out her name as she moved toward them met his ears.

Wes stepped back, relinquishing his hold on her, and instantly felt the chill of his choice.

The realization that he liked having her in his arms was as jarring as pulling up her startled mount. He fought to school his features to one of benign indifference.

But something told him that she could read through it, could read as well as any person opening a book that he had felt the draw they had and was fighting tooth and nail to ignore it.

"Harlow!" Lady Billington gasped as she ran between the horses where they stood. She pulled her sister into her arms, holding her close.

Wes watched the sisters and was thankful that today, at least, the outcome was a good one.

"I'm am well, Lila. Lord Kemsley has ensured that I am so," she said, throwing him a small smile.

He nodded, relief making his limbs feel like he had bolted across the park just as the horse had done. "I'm glad I could be of assistance and here to help." He glanced back in the direction the horse had run from. "Do you know what spooked your mount?" he asked.

"Children playing with a bat and ball, I'm afraid," Lady Billington said. "Oh, Harlow, I was so scared you would fall. Thank heavens you kept your seat and did all you could until Lord Kemsley arrived."

"He is my knight in shining armor," she teased, meeting his gaze quickly. "But truly, I am well, although I do not feel like riding home. May we tie my mount to the back of the carriage?"

"I think that is a sound idea," Wes agreed, not wanting to see Harlow on another horse, not today and perhaps not ever. The fear, the horror clung to his mind, and would not relent.

She could have died. She could have fallen and broken her neck.

A cold chill ran down his spine, and he shivered. "I shall walk you back to the carriage," he said, taking the reins of both horses as they started back toward the equipage.

Harlow walked before him, her sister linking their arms and keeping her younger sister close. He could understand the need as he watched Harlow change the subject about how lovely the day was to try to alleviate her sister's worry.

His concern would last many hours, if not haunt him forever, over what could have happened here today.

TEN

L ater that evening, all of the *ton* were talking about Miss Harlow York's brush with death after her horse bolted in Hyde Park. Not to mention how the gallant hero of the hour, Lord Kemsley, had saved her from absolute death or permanent disablement.

He was no hero. He merely did what any other gentleman would have done should they have seen the horse bolt as he had. That he was the first to react was mere coincidence.

Or at least that is what he told himself when the never-ending, infuriating thought that he cared for Miss York reverberated about in his mind.

He was her friend. They had an agreement. She loved someone else. There was nothing more to his actions today than that of an acquaintance who came to the assistance of another.

He did not have feelings for Harlow York.

He frowned at the amber liquid in his tumbler, and the hairs on the back of his neck lifted. The master of ceremonies continued to call out the names of those arriving at the Frost ball when Lord and Lady Billington and Miss Harlow York were announced.

His gaze lifted across the room, and he watched as she followed her sister and brother-in-law into the already-packed room. This evening she wore a gown of light-green silk overlaid with ornate silver stitching across the bodice. She was a vision, beautiful to a fault, and yet there was more to her than her pretty face and delectable body. She was kind, mischievous, loyal, and had the spontaneity he sometimes lacked when in social situations.

Miss Harlow York was the kind of person one could not help but like, himself included.

She dipped into a curtsy before Lord Hill, the gentleman he had warned her against, but one she continued to allow courtship toward her.

Wes ground his teeth. Was this the gentleman she liked above all others? Was Lord Hill the one she was trying to make jealous and act on that envy by proposing marriage?

That man wasn't fit to wipe her boots, yet he couldn't help but wonder if there were any who were.

He downed his brandy. Such thoughts were not helpful, and he did not need to have them.

He was not going to marry her, so what did he care who she wedded and bedded?

Turning on his heel, he left the room, seeking where Lord and Lady Frost had set up cards and dice games for their guests. He would hibernate in there until he left. Mayhap he would visit Whites on his way home or travel down to the East End to Blackhaven's gaming hell, distracting himself with other feminine company that was safe, not wanting anything from him other than his ability to give them pleasure.

He would not seek out Harlow York this evening. That road led to disaster, and he was still not over visualizing her cold and lifeless form on the grass of Hyde Park should the worst have happened today.

Wes procured another glass of brandy, downing it. Something told him he would need many this evening.

LORD AND LADY FROST'S BALL WAS A crush. Harlow pushed through the crowd, and still, she could not see a few feet in front of her. The room held a smoky haze from the cheap tallow candles her ladyship had chosen to use this evening, much to everyone's dislike and discomfort.

She had made two trips about the room for the past hour, searching for Lord Kemsley, but she could not find him. She paused near a large, ornate fireplace covered with flowers and two gilded columns and frowned.

Had he not come? How was she to pursue him through their lessons if he were not here? For several minutes she debated on what to do. Should she go about the room again?

Seeing Lord Hill heading toward her, she pretended not to see him and joined a group of young ladies she barely knew, hoping he would lose her in the crowd. She was not in the disposition to listen to his many compliments, which for some reason she knew to her very core were false, just a means to trick her into thinking he cared for her.

He did not. The gentlemen here courting her were all the same. Merely doing their duty, finding a wife, giving her babies, and not caring past those facts.

But she did not want a marriage like so many others. She wanted one like her sister, like her good friend Viscountess Leigh.

Her attempt failed, and when he spotted her yet again, she knew what she had to do. Harlow left the ballroom and followed a group of young ladies to the retiring room, deciding that was as good a place as any to hide from Lord Hill. The retiring room had two maids, and several ladies sat for a moment's peace away from the ball below-stairs. Harlow accepted a glass of lemonade and sat beside a window, looking out at the inky blackness.

"Have you seen Lord Kemsley this evening? I did not think a gentleman ever became as foxed as he, but I was wrong," Miss Sweeney said, a mischievous tilt to her lips.

"Mama said it's scandalous of him, but then she also said such actions from the earl are common. He's naughty to the core," Lady Anna Bell, oldest daughter to Lord and Lady Bell, interjected.

Harlow pretended not to hear but couldn't help but wonder where they had seen Lord Kemsley in such a state. She had not been able to locate him anywhere. Had he been avoiding her as she had been avoiding her admirers? The thought was mortifying.

Miss Sweeney chuckled as she stepped from around the screen, where ladies relieved themselves. "He almost fell over coming out of the gambling room Lord and Lady Frost have set up for them all. Not that the Lady Randall seemed to mind. She was more than happy having him lean on her for support."

Harlow stared out the window but could only see her own devastated reflection. She swallowed the lump in her throat. Was Lady Randall skulking about him yet again? She supposed it made sense since the lady was a widow, but Lord Kemsley was not her ladyship's toy. She had married once in her life. It was Harlow's turn now to gain someone's heart.

Her thoughts were absurd and immature, but blast it ... she wanted Kemsley for herself. The thought of Lady Randall, a woman of the world, who no doubt knew how to be with a man more intimately than a kiss, would see Harlow as no threat, nor should she.

Harlow was a country lass from an unknown and untitled family. Wealthy she may be, but she was no dowager with an estate secured by a male heir like Lady Randall was.

"Lord Kemsley did not seem to me to be enjoying Lady Randall's company as much as he once did. If you ask me, he looked distracted, as if he were looking for someone else," Lady Anna stated as she fixed her hair before a mirror.

Harlow's eyes met Lady Anna's through the reflection, and she quickly turned to inspect the gardens. Did Lady Anna mean her? Had she noticed Harlow and Kemsley spending more time together than usual?

The young ladies left, Lady Anna bidding Harlow a good night before shutting the door quietly behind them. Harlow stayed there for several more minutes, not wanting to rejoin the ball, only to see Lady Randall fawning over Kemsley. That he was foxed would only make the vision worse as he would probably forget all about their lessons and be too busy trying to get under her ladyship's skirt than to seek her out.

Anger mixed with frustration thrummed through her, and she left the room and stormed down the corridor. She stopped at the top of the stairs, not wanting to look like some crazed lovesick jealous fool.

He did not know she wanted him. Adored and cared for him, and nor would she give her game away yet. To do so would mean he would run and keep from her, which was the last result she wished to procure.

Just then, a footman strolled from the ball and stepped outside. Harlow remained at the top of the stairs. She wasn't sure what halted her steps, but something told her to wait, to pause and watch.

The tinkering laugh of Lady Randall burst into the foyer before her ladyship, and Lord Kemsley stumbled into the foyer from the ballroom, a footman handing her ladyship her shawl.

A carriage rolled to a stop before the town house door, and with sickening dread, Harlow watched as Lord Kemsley escorted Lady Randall out of the house and down the steps.

Only then did Harlow move toward the ground floor. She paused on the bottom step, and dread—a sickening lump of stone settled in her chest—descended as she watched him help Lady Randall climb up in the carriage.

Before joining her, he turned, and their gazes met.

His eyes widened seeing her, and he took a step toward her before Lady Randall's voice halted his direction.

All her vocation, the many weeks of trying to make him see her for more than what she was to him, a friend, fell away and crumbled at her feet. He did not care for her at all. Not if he were escaping Lord and Lady Frost's ball to rut with Lady Randall.

Harlow wanted to shout, "whore," but then that was beneath her, and her ladyship was no light-skirt.

She thought she read regret and maybe hesitation on Kemsley's face before he turned and joined her ladyship in the carriage. The smug, arrogant smirk from Lady Randall, however, was not missed, and Harlow knew she believed she had finally won the war between them both.

Not willing to watch them depart, Harlow tipped her nose into the air, attempting to appear above both their actions, and returned to the ball. That her heart hurt and her vision blurred were irrelevant, and at least something that Lord Kemsley had not seen.

Eleven

Wes's stomach was in knots. He fought not to look over his shoulder as Lord and Lady Frost's town house disappeared along the London street as the carriage rolled down Piccadilly.

"I'm so glad that you sought me out, my lord. I have missed you these past weeks," Lady Randall said, sultriness dripping from her tone. "Where shall we go? Yours or mine?" she asked him, her breast pushed up hard against his arm.

The feeling of her plump, willing body did little to spark expectation. When he had stumbled upon her ladyship at the ball, for a moment relief had poured through him that it was not Miss York. He did not want to see Harlow, was scared that the emotions that had bombarded him this afternoon in the park would return.

He ought to feel nothing but relief that his

friend was safe. Miss York was nothing to him but a student in the art of seduction.

His being seduced by her was not part of the scheme.

"Yours," he said, steeling himself to move forward with his impromptu plan this evening to lose himself in Lady Randall's willing body, forget about the light-brown-haired, green-eyed lass that haunted his dreams.

She looked so devastated by his leaving this evening.

Wes closed his eyes, not wanting to remember such detail. He had hoped to leave without anyone noticing. He had not thought the very woman he had been avoiding all evening would be the one to catch him.

He had never felt so small and guilty in his life.

"I have so much planned for us, Wes. Everything that you like, I'm more than willing to accommodate." She leaned up, her lips brushing his cheek, and he stilled.

He could not do this.

In the past, he probably would have tupped her in the carriage before reaching their destination, but not anymore. Not tonight. The idea held no allure, and he knew who to blame for that.

Harlow ...

The carriage rolled to a halt before Lady Randall's town house, and a footman jumped down, opening the door. He helped her ladyship alight but then paused at the threshold of the carriage door. "I'm afraid I'm no longer going to be able to accompany you, my lady. My sincerest apologies. Goodnight," he said, ignoring the shocked visage of her ladyship and his footman, who knew from his past rendezvous what occurred and would not have expected Wes to turn down such an opportunity.

"But I thought ..." she said, raising her chin similar to how Harlow had done when the truth of the situation before her came clear. "Good evening, Lord Kemsley. Thank you for escorting me home," she said, turning on her heel without a backward glance.

"Home," he ordered his driver, slumping onto the squabs. He ignored the little voice in his head to turn back and rut Harlow York out of his mind.

But even then, he knew she would not budge from the position she now held. She was imprinted there after their kiss, and damn it all to hell, she would not dissipate.

HARLOW WAS THANKFUL WHEN HER sister left to go shopping on Bond Street, leaving her to rusticate and wallow in her own self-pity the following morning. She had slept little overnight. Images of Lord Kemsley locked in the arms of Lady Randall haunted both her sleeping and waking hours.

How dare he?

But then, why not dare he? He was a bachelor, not courting anyone. No matter how much she may wish he were courting her, he was not. He owed her nothing.

But that kiss ...

There was something about their kiss that had been different than mere instruction. He had lost control. She was sure of it. He had wanted her, not merely to teach.

She was not wrong about that.

Harlow all but stomped her way down the stairs and hid at the back of the house in a small room that held no purpose at all, although it was still comfortable as all the others, sporting an opulent settee and an outlook on the back gardens, as limited as the one window was.

A knock sounded on the door, and she bid the footman entry.

"Miss York, a Lord Kemsley to see you," he announced.

Harlow turned from glaring at the outdoor rose bushes to find Lord Kemsley striding into the room, making a determined line toward her.

"Miss York, good morning. I hope you do not mind me calling on you," he said, all sweet words, as if butter would not melt on his cheating, Lady Randall-tupping mouth.

She frowned at her thoughts. Could you tup with your mouth? She did not think so, but even so, he was the last person she wished to see today.

"Lord Kemsley, you're here. I would have thought you would have been much engaged elsewhere," she said, raising one sarcastic brow, hoping he would read more into her words than their face value.

The little flexing of the muscle in his jaw told her he had. "We have lessons, Miss York. Do not tell me you have forgotten?"

She brushed past him, moving to sit on the settee. "We no longer need such lessons. You are a busy man, sought out by many. I'm merely getting in your way of enjoying your Season." The words tasted like vinegar. She did not want to say them. It hurt to admit that as much as she knew this predicament, this pain she was feeling was all her own doing.

She should never have tried to win his love and affection. She was a fool to have thought her plan would work.

He came and sat beside her, leaning back on the settee as if he owned the house. Such an obnoxious, blind man who could not read the room.

"I did not sleep with Lady Randall," he blurted.

Harlow could feel his gaze on her, and she fought not to react to his admission. Had he not slept with her ladyship? Relief poured through her. At least maybe there was a little chance she could still win his heart.

But that he had gone in the first place with the Lady Randall told her she had further to go to win him completely. "I do not believe I need to know such things, my lord. What you do in your private life is none of my concern."

He threw her a disbelieving look. "Do you mean that? Last night at the Frost ball, you looked upset at my departure with her ladyship. I escorted her home. As you know, we're old friends, nothing else."

Harlow shrugged and kept her attention on the window that looked out over the garden, not Lord Kemsley. His gaze burned a path upon her cheek, but still, she would not look at him. If she did so, she knew with certainty he would guess all her thoughts and feelings, and that would never do.

While she would like to be his wife one day, she would not give him so much power over her just yet. He needed to earn her love, if he ever wished to, and to expose herself now, what she was feeling, hurt, anger, jealousy, would not do her well at all.

"Very well, what lessons did you have in mind for today?" she asked, schooling her features.

"More kissing? Dancing? Or was there something else you wanted to show me, my lord?"

Lord Kemsley narrowed his eyes before a small, knowing smile spread across his lips. "I want to talk about the power of a touch, Miss York."

"Touch?" she blurted, not too pleased about the idea. Sounded rather boring to her. "You want to hold my hand, and that's how you will teach me to win over my desired love?" she scoffed. "I do not think these lessons are helping at all."

"On the contrary," he said. "A touch can be very powerful indeed, sensual also, and could give the man you wish to marry the insight he may require to know that you're the one for him. A touch," he said, taking her hand and laying it within his, "could be the catalyst that shows him you wish for more than mere friendship."

Harlow ignored that her heart thumped quicker in her chest and fought to look indifferent. "Very well, show me how a touch could alter everything between a man and woman."

"My pleasure." His thumb brushed the top of her hand. His attention focused on where they joined. "Your hands, Miss York are so very soft. Your fingers are long and thin, most delicate." He lifted her hand to his lips and brushed his mouth softly against the top of her hand, sending shivers down her spine. She swallowed, not expecting her body to betray her when she was so determined to be angry at Lord Kemsley forever.

He met her gaze, his fingers playing with hers for several minutes, the corner of his eyes crinkled, and the breath in her lungs seized. He was so handsome, virile, and wicked. Her body betrayed her. She ached for his touch, not just on her hand, but everywhere. Even places no upstanding, unmarried lady of society should want. He entwined their fingers, palm to palm, and she gasped. "Together just so," he said. "Do you not feel how close we are? How everything, even the air in the room, is thicker with awareness?"

Harlow nodded, daring not to speak in case she begged him to touch her everywhere else on her person.

"And if I pull you close, slip the shoulder of your gown a little to the side and kiss your skin here," he said, his lips pressing down on her shoulder. His mouth moved along her collarbone, and without thought, she clasped the nape of his neck, holding him there.

Her breath came in quick succession, and his kisses against her neck became more pressing, urgent.

"Your scent." He groaned into her ear, and she closed her eyes, wanting this moment to last forever. "Roses, so sweet, so intoxicating."

Harlow opened her eyes just as he pulled back. Their gazes met, held, and desire, hot and strong, tore through her. "Where else can a man touch a woman?" she asked, needing to know if the naughty books she had read in the past were indeed possible.

Weakness burned in his gaze. "Here," he said, his hand slipping along her waist to cup one breast. "And if I squeeze you a little, find the sensitive pebble hiding beneath all that muslin," he said, doing as he instructed, "and I roll my thumb over it just so it'll pucker into a little button."

Harlow moaned when he did as he said, her body afire and wanting him with a need she did not understand but wanted to.

Desperately.

"I like how that feels," she whispered, pushing into his hand. "And if I allow the man I wish to marry to do this to me, you believe it'll bring us closer? Make him want me as his wife?"

"He will think upon the matter more than he has with anyone else," Kemsley said, pulling back and dropping her from his hold.

Harlow let out a yelp of displeasure before she remembered this was only a lesson for him, but was it?

The muscle in his jaw told another tale altogether.

"Well," she said, forcing her voice to be unaffected, even if her heart and body ached for nothing but the man before her. "Let us hope he does come to his senses soon before I give up on my quest and marry someone else. Regret is a terrible mistress, and I would hate for the man I adore to settle for anything that is less than what he could have."

Lord Kemsley met her eyes but nodded in agreement, even if he appeared as if he wanted to say something else, argue her point.

"You are right, of course. Do what I instructed you today, and you'll be one more step closer to getting what you want." He stood and bowed. "I have an appointment, forgive me, but I must leave. Good day, Miss York," he said, striding from the room before she could utter a reply.

A grin lifted her lips as she watched him disappear into the passageway. "Good day, Lord Kemsley," she called after him, knowing he would not have heard. "And good luck not being affected by me more than you already are."

TWELVE

Wes could not get home quickly enough. What was the hell wrong with him? He could not turn up on Miss York's doorstep and then do whatever the hell he wanted with her.

That being a hell of a lot after kissing her neck. He had wanted to lift up her skirts right there and then in her sister's house and touch her where he knew she ached.

Wes thrust the thought aside, slamming through the front door of his lodgings and storming up the stairs. He dismissed his valet, who met him along the first-floor landing. He told him he would not be needed this evening and locked himself away in his room.

Relief poured through him that he was alone, his door locked where no one could interrupt him. He stripped off his jacket and cravat, throwing them onto the floor before ripping off his shirt.

His cock stood to attention, hard and aching for Harlow York.

Damn it all to hell. What was he going to do?

Well, he knew what he was going to do. He lay on his bed and ripped his falls open. His erection sprang free, and relief and expectation thrummed through him when his fingers wrapped hard about his cock.

He closed his eyes, all his thoughts on what he had wanted to do to Harlow just minutes before.

Imaginings of stripping her gown down past her breasts, laving her, teasing the rosy beaded buds haunted his mind. He stroked his cock harder, wishing he were between her legs, teasing her cunny with his cock before he thrust inside her sweet, hot quim.

Wes groaned and spent hard and long atop his stomach. His breathing ragged, he lay there for several minutes, enjoying the thought, the euphoria he would experience should he gain what he wanted.

To have Harlow beneath him on this bed, his to command, to take, to give pleasure to until she could not stand thinking about anyone else but him at her side.

"Fuck," he swore, tumbling from the bed. He picked up his shirt and wiped his stomach before ringing for his valet. He would bathe and apologize to his manservant for dismissing him early and then changing his mind.

He needed to attend the Collins ball this evening. He would seek out Harlow and explain to her that their lessons were no longer a good idea. That his tutelage today had gone too far, that he was a rogue to his very core, and it was unlikely he would not try to persuade her to give him more of herself.

He cringed, unlocked the door, and hated himself for the thought. She loved someone else. He could not tup her and then allow her to ride off into the sunset with some random gentleman.

Something told him that he would want her even if she married and said her vows to another. He was the devil's spawn.

"You rang, my lord?" his valet said before slipping into the room and picking up after his mess.

"Yes, apologies, Peter, but I require a bath and will need help dressing for the Collins ball this evening. You will not need to stay up to attend to me when I return."

"Of course, my lord," Peter said. "I shall organize your bath posthaste."

Wes sighed when his door closed, leaving him alone. What would he do with this need? How would he keep from her, even if he stopped their lessons?

Did he have so little control that he could not

abide by the rules of society and keep his hands to himself? Of course, he could, he was a man, and men were warriors, fighters, and certainly not suspectable to emotions and feelings.

Blast and hell, he would not stoop so low. Not even for the delectable Harlow York.

HARLOW ENSURED SHE WORE THE MOST scandalous gown for this evening's ball. As an unmarried maid, bright colors were frowned upon, and so she had dressed in the darkest shade of emerald green she could without raising a judgemental eye from the matrons of the *ton*.

Tonight she would not allow Lord Kemsley out of her sight without stealing him away first and granting herself another kiss.

After this afternoon, she had been left hot and bothered, her lips tingling with a need that was not sated. That he had kissed her everywhere else but her mouth was maddening.

She breathed deeply and closed her eyes a moment, thinking of his lips brushing the sensitive skin beneath the lobe of her ear.

"I can only guess who you're thinking of right at this moment," Isla said, grinning as she passed Harlow a glass of ratafia.

"I just thought that the gentlemen here ought to wash more. Do you not think it smells a little stale in here?" she hedged. There were certain things she could tell her friend, and then there were other things that she could not.

Although she wasn't certain if Isla would be horrified if she knew what Harlow had done so far with Lord Kemsley, being as uncertain as she was, she could not risk her friend advising against her lessons since they were progressing so well.

"Oh, there is Duke. I shall return in but a moment," her friend said, already moving toward her husband.

Such love shone between them the moment Lord Leigh spied Isla. She wanted the same. A love match. Was that too much to ask?

For several minutes she stood alone, lost in her thoughts and watching as the ballroom slowly filled with guests. True to her word, Isla returned soon after, two glasses of champagne in her hand.

She handed Harlow one. "Right, my darling friend, I demand to know what has happened between you and Lord Kemsley since the Season commenced. I've known you since we were children and watching you just now, you have the same expression as you did when you stole strawberries from the elder Mrs. Bagshaw's garden and gave yourself a stomach ache from eating them all with the greatest glee," Isla stated, watching her keenly.

Should Harlow tell her more than she had

already? They had never kept secrets before, and she had to tell someone, or she would go mad. "I've kissed Lord Kemsley," she blurted. "But only because of the lessons in seduction he's giving me. You know I asked him to instruct me in those ways so I may win the heart of the man I wish to marry, which of course, is him." The words tumbled from her mouth and would not stop. "But something is different. There has been a change between us, and I'm terrified that the change means more to me than to his lordship."

"Well, that is a lot to digest," Isla said, her eyes wide. "Lord Kemsley is here, you know. I've been watching his lordship, and he seems to be hiding from you in a reflective kind of way, but also unable to take his gaze from you."

Hope blossomed through her at her friend's words, along with despair. "Do you think this means that my application to win his heart this way may be working? To me, that does sound like he's a little confused, if not smitten."

Isla chuckled, coming to stand beside her and nodding in a direction across the room. "Over there, my dear. Near Lady Fairchild, whom he's trying to hide behind."

Harlow studied where Isla stated and, sure enough, found Lord Kemsley behind her ladyship, except he did not look pensive and concerned to her. No, not in the least.

He looked rightfully deadly.

His gaze burned a path through the multitude of guests, and Harlow felt the lick of heat right to her core.

Her belly fluttered, and she sipped her champagne. "I want him," she admitted. "In a way that I've never wanted anyone before. I cannot breathe or think without wishing him near. He is in my mind night and day, and all I can think about are his lips upon me, and not just on my mouth."

"Well," Isla gasped, flicking open her fan and waving it before her face. "He sounds like he kisses very well if that is what you think of him."

"Oh yes, he does. I lose my ability to think clearly when I'm in his arms. If I do not marry him, I will never be happy. He is a match to my soul even if he is so very stubborn at present and does not know that fact."

Isla smiled. "I think you may be right." She paused, both of them watching Lord Kemsley, who had been found by the Lady Fairchild and was currently held prisoner, as she introduced him to her debutante niece.

Harlow chuckled at the sight. He appeared decidedly uncomfortable, like he did not want to be there at all. He glanced across the room and met her gaze, and like a bolt of lightning, Harlow felt his gaze like a physical touch.

Her skin prickled, and a sense of expectation thrummed through her blood. A feeling that no matter the lessons, no matter how much he declared he did not want to marry anyone, there would be nothing stopping either of them from getting what they wanted.

Each other.

THIRTEEN

The moment Wes spied Miss York at the Bridges' ball, an overwhelming realization morphed in his mind.

He wanted her.

Maybe he did not want a wife and was not ready for such commitments, but hell, he enjoyed their lessons. Only hours before he decided he would not continue with them, but seeing Harlow again, he knew his adamant stance would not hold.

He wanted her in his bed.

However, the question remained. Would she allow such liberties knowing he did not want a lifelong commitment? He doubted she would. No lady of delicate means such as herself would ever allow such privileges, and he could not help but think what a shame that fact was.

He would take liberties if he could and enjoy

every single one of them, and she too, he would wager.

Lady Fairchild droned on about her niece's abilities and suitability to being a man's wife. He smiled and nodded, pretending to be interested as Miss Cullen, too, joined in with her aunt's praises, but he was not invested.

All he wanted was to go to Harlow, whose eyes remained locked on him, burning a path across the room that made his skin prickle with heat.

That he had lit the fire within her sent a longing roaring through him that he wanted to stoke, see how hot he could make her burn.

"If you will excuse me," he said partway through Lady Fairchild stating how many children Miss Cullen had agreed to bear should she find a match.

He broke free, striding toward Miss York. He ignored other attempts from the numerous mamas who tried to gain his attention. Only one woman here this evening interested him, and no one else.

"Good evening, Lady Leigh, Miss York," he said, bowing. He met Harlow's gaze, and a small smile lifted the corners of his lips, no matter how hard he tried to remain aloof before their friends.

"Lord Kemsley, good evening. We did not think you would free yourself so soon from Lady Fairchild. She is not known for allowing eligible young men to escape her clutches, not once she has you within her grip," the viscountess teased, grinning along with Harlow.

He liked seeing her smile. When they had parted at the Collins ball, and she had caught him with Lady Randall, the pain etched on her normally pretty features had burned his heart to a cinder.

"I'm very good at escaping, my lady."

She raised one brow. "That is not what I've heard," she quipped. "If you'll excuse me, my husband is calling me to him." She left Harlow and himself alone before Harlow could utter one excuse to leave with her.

After what they had done at her home earlier this afternoon, he was not sure what kind of reception she would greet him with, but something told him no matter how nervous she was, she welcomed his company.

"And so we're alone again," he teased.

"Not for long, my lord. I'm about to dance with Lord Abercromby," she said as his lordship bowed before them both and took Harlow's hand, leading her away from him.

For a moment, Wes stood watching them before a few curious eyes turned in his direction. He could read the interest, see the cogs in their minds turning, trying to figure out what was happening between him and Miss York.

That he could not answer himself, but what

he did know was he disliked the wide smile and bright eyes she had turned on to charm the viscount.

Perhaps he was the fellow she wanted to marry? He narrowed his eyes and strolled along the edge of the ballroom, keeping checks as to where Miss York was at all times, but not so much so that others noticed.

Thankfully, the dance ended just as he had made one loop of the ballroom. Disappointment stabbed him at the sight of Harlow being whisked out again for another dance with a different gentleman.

By the time two hours had passed and many dance partners later, Wes's patience was wearing thin. He needed to speak to her. Hell, he needed to be alone with her if only to remind her of their lessons, which he now firmly believed were far from over.

"You look a little lost, my lord. Where is Lady Randall?" Harlow asked at his side, without his realizing she was there. "Surely she is hovering about just waiting for you to escort her home yet again," she said, her tone tinged with venom.

"I told you today, Miss York, that we are friends and nothing more. I would not be waiting for you if I did not think higher of our friendship than hers. We have lessons to attend."

Miss York raised her brow in disbelief. "We had our lessons today, and I thank you for them.

I should like the man I wish to marry to kiss my neck as you did. When you were kissing me," she whispered, "I pictured you as him, and it made the instruction all the more enjoyable."

Wes felt his eye twitch at her words. She imagined him as someone else? How the hell had he managed to do that, to allow such a vile thing to happen?

But then, wasn't that the point? As much as he enjoyed having her in his arms, kissing her sweet lips, he did not want to marry, not now, at least. He was far too young for that and too much of a rake to settle down with one lady for the remainder of his life. He would be bored within a month. His brother had done his duty to the family already, begetting a son, so the urgency for him to settle had waned.

She would be safer marrying another, but the thought left a sour taste in his mouth.

"Very good," he agreed, as much as the words pained him. "We should continue our lessons then. My instruction seems to be working. You've certainly been busy this evening with the ball. Why I have not seen you without a partner these past two hours," he stated, hoping the ire in his tone was not discernible.

Her smug visage told him he had failed at hiding his annoyance. "I have, have I not? Most sought after, and the night is still young. I merely wished for a glass of lemonade." She stared up at him as if he ought to produce such a repast immediately, and damn her little minx soul. He wanted to do as she asked without delay.

Instead, he stared back at her, but somewhere between their standoff, her eyes softened, and his heart kicked up a beat. He swallowed, stepping closer, desire licking at the back of his neck and whispering all the naughty, delicious things he wanted to do with her if only he could get her alone.

"What did you wish for our lessons to be about this evening, Lord Kemsley?" she whispered, innocence dripping from lips he knew could be wicked.

"I wish to have supper with you. My instruction this evening involves food and how it can help you gain the hand of the man you wish to marry."

"Food?" she asked, her tone one of disbelief. "Do be serious, Lord Kemsley. If you do not wish to continue with my lessons, you can merely be honest and tell me so."

"No," he added quickly. "I do not jest. Meet me in the supper room when it is announced. We shall dine together, and you will see what I mean."

She shrugged just as Lord Hill came to claim her hand in a dance. "Very well, my lord. I shall see you at supper as you wish."

* * *

It seemed to take an age for supper to be served, and not only was Harlow hungry, her stomach rumbling at inappropriate times, but she wanted to see what Lord Kemsley meant by his food lessons.

She could not understand what he could mean by this narrative, but she would supper with him and listen. Maybe what he explained would help her seduce the maddening man who refused to buckle to her charms.

She located Lord Kemsley at a table for two near a secluded corner of the supper room, an abundance of treats already set out before him as he waited for her.

Harlow sat without a word and looked over the portions he had chosen for them. A bowl of cut-up lobster, *Charlotte Russe à la Vanille*, decorated ham, Savoy Cake, fruit tarts, a slice of cheesecake, a small dish of various summer fruits, and two glasses of lemonade, just as she had mentioned earlier. She calmed her features, not wanting him to know the pleasure that filled her that he remembered what she had wanted to drink.

"A lovely, delicious spread, my lord. Now show me how you think food can help me with my quest." She picked up her glass of lemonade and took a sip.

He threw her a knowing grin before picking up a strawberry from the bowl of fruits. "Seducing a man does not have to be just tactile or imperceptible, Miss York. You can gain advantage from a look across the room, a stolen kiss to the lips, and other places on the body as I've shown, but food too, can be used in your armory."

"Really? Do tell." She watched him study the strawberry in his hand before placing it in his mouth. He closed his lips about the fruit in a manner she'd never studied before. He kept his eyes upon her, biting into the berry before closing them as if it were the tastiest, sweetest fruit in the world.

Harlow couldn't help but think right at this moment, the strawberry was indeed just that.

"Having you watch me, I can accentuate how I eat supper. I can exaggerate my pleasure with the fruit even more, watch." He picked up another strawberry, this time groaning, making her stomach flutter low and deep inside.

"Let me try," she said, wanting to see if he would react the way she was to watching him snack on fruits and other good things. She reached for a spoon and the jelly he had procured for them. Scooping up a spoonful, she opened her mouth, keeping her eyes on him as she placed the jelly into her mouth before closing her lips over the spoon.

"Now pull the spoon out slowly between your lips," he whispered, clearing his throat.

Harlow did as he advised, pulling the spoon

slowly from her mouth before licking it to ensure she had eaten every bite. "How was that?" she said, spooning up another bit of jelly.

"Very good, now do it again, but slower," he instructed, his attention fixed on her lips.

His swallow was almost audible and pleasure coursed through her blood that what she was doing, what he was advising, was having as much effect on him as it was on her.

Maybe Kemsley had not been teasing when he brought food into their lessons.

Harlow slipped more jelly into her mouth and closed her eyes. She let out a little moan of delight just as he had done before pulling the spoon slowly from between her lips.

His eyes burned across the table at her and her stomach gave another delicious flip. She watched him as he watched her, and Harlow knew he felt as she did to her very core. As if she were off-center, as if the world was about to change direction, but for the better.

"Now, eat a fruit tart," he demanded with a low, gravelly voice.

Harlow fought not to grin and picked up the small blackberry tart. These were small, bite-sized, and perfect for balls and parties. She licked her lips, opening her mouth before placing it on her tongue. She closed her lips, chewing slowly while she watched Kemsley. He leaned back in his chair and adjusted his cravat before running a hand through his hair.

"Hmmm," she moaned. "These are delicious, my lord. You ought to try one. They're very moist," she explained, swallowing before gifting him a mischievous grin.

"I think that ought to conclude our lesson," he stated, the muscle twitching on his jaw again.

"Oh really?" She pouted. Now that she knew where he was going with these food lessons, she did not want them to end. Not only was she hungry, and the food was welcome, but she liked seeing him all flustered and at sea. What she was doing was working, certainly on Lord Kemsley.

He wanted her. She could read it in his eyes as clearly as she could see the deep blue that burned back at her. "But I'm enjoying tonight's lesson. It's most valuable."

"Do you want to know why watching a woman eat just as you have been will drive the man you wish to marry beyond his endurance?" he asked.

Harlow leaned forward, reaching under the table to place her hand on his knee. The muscle under her palm tightened before his hand came to lay atop hers, holding her there. "I think I know what the outcome of the lesson is about, my lord. I can see that your instruction has been so victorious that it has succeeded even with you."

His fingers entwined with hers on his knee, and he smirked. His lordship leaned forward, bringing them closer still. "Watching a woman eat reminds a man of certain things you shall only do with your husband. He will think of that when he watches you, imagines other things instead of the food you just ate, and he will be malleable in your hands, do whatever you wish, whenever you wish it."

"Really?" she said, raising her brow. "And if I wish for my lessons to continue this evening, may we go over the kissing portion of your tutelage? Would you be amenable to my request?"

He watched her for a moment, his attention darting to the others in the supper room before meeting hers. "I would," he said. "Revision is all part of learning."

Harlow nodded. "Very true indeed."

FOURTEEN

Do not do it reverberated in Wes's mind, but he could not heed the warning in his head. Watching Harlow learn the art of seduction through food had his body overriding his common sense.

He had to kiss her. Had to taste those sweet lips that had taunted him to no end this past half hour.

"The house is full of guests, and many are coming and going upstairs to the retiring room. I'm not certain we can sneak away here without being seen," he said, knowing that he would not heed his advice and keep from her.

She raised one determined brow. "A closet sits a little way up from the retiring room. I saw a maid taking linens from there when I used the room earlier. I will slip into that room instead of the retiring room by mistake. I expect to see you there," she said, pinning him to his chair with a look that promised so much. Pleasure more than anything else, desire too, flickered in her green eyes.

Wes watched her saunter away, her hips swinging in a seductive dance that he knew she did not even realize she was doing. Harlow spoke to several friends as the ball commenced again, and people slowly emptied the supper room.

For a moment he walked about the ballroom doing the same, speaking to acquaintances and watching the dancing, but his mind was elsewhere. Namely, Harlow, who stood across the ballroom floor, her laughter ringing out when she found something funny said by the Duchess of Derby.

She was so pretty, and charming, not to mention more forward and wicked than he first thought her. He liked her more and more with every passing moment they spent in each other's company.

And in a few short minutes, he would kiss her again.

He excused himself, striding from the room, not waiting to see if Harlow took heed of his departure. She would join him soon, and that was enough to keep his pace and direction sound.

It was not hard to find the linen closet, and before closing the door, he took in his surroundings. Three walls with shelves and a small folding table made up the room. No other light could penetrate the room once the door was closed, and he noted no lock from the inside. Not that there should be, but he could only hope no one needed any linens for the few moments he would have alone with her.

He closed the door, happy that no one came upon the passageway, and waited. His body thrummed with expectation, his stomach in knots, all things he was not used to feeling when waiting for a woman.

And he had many of those during his six and twenty years. Desire he felt, pleasure and relief, but something about this night, waiting for Harlow, was different.

His emotions were heightened. Everything was intensified, and impatience niggled at his nerves, taunting him.

He slumped against the folding table and crossed his arms, wondering how long she would be. He hoped she would not be prolonged.

THE FOLLOWING DAY HARLOW STILL could not stop laughing at the little revenge she had played on Lord Kemsley. She sat in the gardens at her sister's house, surrounded by large trees and hedges that the previous Viscounts of Billington had painstakingly grown and nurtured during the hundreds of years the family held the title.

From her location, she could only see the rooftop of her sister's house and nothing else. She placed down the book of love poetry—Byron really was ideal when one was feeling a little reflective—and stared up at the fluffy white clouds billowing and passing above. For several minutes she tried to see animal shapes within them but only managed to see a bird fly overhead instead.

"This is not the linen cupboard," a decidedly annoyed and deep baritone growled from behind her.

Harlow gasped and sat up, turning to find Lord Kemsley glaring at her. The frustration on his visage flickered to life her masked desire for the man, and she chuckled. "Were you waiting long? I'm so very sorry I could not make our rendezvous after all. Something came up," she explained. Nothing of the sort did. She did not want to do what he wished, what they both expected, not after she had seen him leave with Lady Randall the night before without a by-your-leave.

She forced herself not to grind her teeth at the thought of them together.

"I will admit it took me several minutes, thirty, in fact, to realize that you were not coming."

She laughed, unable to hold it in a moment longer, and stared up at him. "Are you so very angry at me, my lord?" she asked.

He came and sat beside her, lying on her blanket and staring at the clouds as she had done. "Kiss me now, and all is forgiven."

Harlow turned to face him and felt the shock crossing her face. "I cannot do that, and nor should you be lying on my blanket. What if someone sees us?"

"You had the opportunity last evening to be alone, secluded, to learn a little more in the art of kissing, and instead, you chose to stay at the ball." He narrowed his eyes at her. "When did you decide to leave me in the cupboard like a dirty secret?"

"The moment I left the supper room." She leaned over him, placing her hands on either side of his head. "But here is not the place to be kissing each other either." She ran one finger over his jaw and felt the stubble pricking her finger before rubbing her thumb across his bottom lip. So soft, so damn kissable that it hurt. "That will have to be for another time, my lord."

She went to leave, and he sat up, clasping her about the waist, and before she could utter a word of refusal, he had her flat on her back, his hard, heavy body crushing her into the soft grass beneath the blanket.

"This is a perfect enough time. Do you know what I did when I returned home, Miss York?" he asked her.

She shook her head, swallowing the nerves he

ignited at the burning desire in his eyes. "I thought about all the things I was going to do to you for missing a lesson. I thought of spanking your ass," he said, reaching behind her, his hand clasping one of her bottom cheeks and squeezing it.

Hard.

She gasped, but it came out more as a moan, and his eyes darkened further. "I thought about calling on you last night here, stealing into the house, and making you beg for forgiveness with all sorts of wild and wicked things."

Harlow nodded, wanting those sinful ideas to come true. Wanting him to do it now. Was he game enough? Would he try to kiss her, touch her out in the gardens where anyone could come upon them?

"What exactly would you do to punish me?" she asked him, hoping he would show her everything he taunted her with. For he was teasing her, making her feel things she never had before, and he was well aware of the effect.

His hand slipped over her hip, and the cool kiss of air touched her ankle, followed by her knee, and then her thigh. She did not try to stop his fondling. His large, warm hand slid against the skin on her inner thigh, and shivers ran through her body.

"I want to make you feel how I felt last evening. Unsatisfied," he breathed against her lips, so close that if she leaned forward just a little bit, she could kiss him.

His hand cupped her mons, and she ought to feel disgusted, embarrassed for how utterly damp she was, but she did not. Without thinking, as if her body instinctively knew, she pushed into his touch, his fingers playing her like a delicate instrument.

Harlow moaned when his thumb rolled against one particular spot, his other fingers teasing her cunny.

She could not wait and reached up, pulling him down to kiss her. His mouth covered hers, hungry and demanding. Their tongues tangled, teeth nipped, and moans mingled as he lay against her, his touch, his mouth in control of her in all ways.

Like the wanton she was, she spread her legs farther, needing him, wanting him, not just his hand. He kissed her neck, murmuring unintelligible things against her skin.

She held on to him, her body on fire, on a precipice she knew would be worth the climb.

"Wes," she begged, using his given name for the first time. "What kind of lesson is this?" she asked.

He pulled back, his eyes wild, his hair askew. Never had she seen him so disheveled and so desirable all at once. Her heart lurched, and she was lost.

She was utterly and devotedly in love with him.

Realization dawned, and she saw the exact moment he realized what he was doing and where. He wrenched out of her hold and flicked her gown down with more ability than she wanted to think about right now. Not wanting to know how many women he may have lain with like this within his six and twenty years.

He stood, staring down at her as if he did not know where he was or who he was with. "Apologies. I have pressed our lesson too far. Forgive me," he said, striding across the lawn, behind shrubbery, and out of view.

Harlow sat up, staring in the direction he walked, not quite sure what had just happened, but knowing it was profound. On her behalf, in any case. And mayhap his as well. He wanted to teach her a lesson. Leave her as unsatisfied as he had been last night.

Well, perhaps he had been left just so yet again, and this time under his own steam.

FIFTEEN

W es was in trouble. Big trouble with a capital *H*. He had called on Harlow, determined to punish her, chastise her for making him look like the fool.

Instead, he had mauled her, almost ripped his breeches down, and satisfied them both on the ground like some heathen.

He ran a hand through his hair. What the hell was wrong with him? How could he have lost control as he had?

Their lessons had gone too far, but now, he could not stop them. Nor did he want to. He wanted her. Wanted to make her come either by hand, tongue, or both.

The idea caused heat to lick up his spine, and he groaned.

"The carriage is ready, my lord," his valet said, coming into his library where he had ensconced himself since leaving Harlow's home earlier that day.

He glanced at the brandy decanter, now almost empty, and knew he ought not to attend the Bridges ball—held yearly in the London pleasure gardens of Vauxhall—but nor could he stay home.

His thoughts on Harlow would indeed drive him to distraction, and he needed to attend, be by her side, and ensure she was safe in such a location.

Safe from whom? You?

He ignored the warning voice and left his town house, using the time in the carriage to Mount Street to breathe deep and try to force himself to sober up.

It did not take him long to reach the gardens, and already the ball was in full swing. People danced while others dined in the many supper boxes that sat about the park overlooking the outdoor ballroom.

As if his eyes were attuned to her, he spied Harlow dancing with Lord Poulett. He stood beside a tree, watching her weave in and out of other dancers, laughing and smiling, and all he could think about was the delicious sounds she made in his arms this afternoon.

How well she fit against him.

She was so beautiful that his heart ached. He ran a hand through his hair, wondering what the bollocks was happening to him. Why he was feeling all at sea and disillusioned. He did not want a wife. He had promised himself that he would not look for a bride to ensure his family name and line until he absolutely had to.

But he was only six and twenty, not ready to promise himself to only one woman for the rest of his life like his brother had done.

Not that he was even certain that he could.

He cringed. Nor could he stomach hurting her, which being unfaithful would surely do.

The dance came to an end, and she dipped into a curtsy, laughing up at something his lordship said before her attention swept over the crowd and she saw him.

Like a blow to his stomach, he felt her gaze slam into him, and he took a deep breath. He would need to choose. To decide if he were willing to give up all his assertions and his pursuits and fight for a woman who loved another.

For all her ability, when he had her alone, her kisses and touch did not mean she wanted him as a husband in return. She saw him as a teacher, someone to guide her toward the one man she wanted.

Lord Poulett and Abercromby more than most of late, and he couldn't help but believe that one of them was the man she intended to marry.

The thought left a sour taste in his mouth

and moved his attention to Harlow. He was not ready to play his hand just yet.

She, however, did not seem to heed his attempt at disinterest and excused herself before joining him under the tree.

"Lord Poulett is very attentive of late. I do believe your assistance these past weeks is working, my lord. And after today's lesson, well, I'm certain that should he ask me to marry him, and I agree, our betrothal will be a pleasurable four weeks indeed."

Wes shut his mouth with a snap and fought not to swear. "Do let me know if you require more instruction, Miss York. We're outdoors this evening, which seems conducive to a successful lesson," he teased, wanting to remind her of today when she had been in his arms. That it was his lips that had been on her person, his hand against her wet mons. Not Lord Whatever His Name Was.

The thought made his cock hard, and he took a deep breath, needing to keep a cool head. At least when it came to the one sitting on his shoulders.

"I thought that I may try to incorporate what you have taught me with Lord Poulett. Now that you seem to have guessed my intended, there is no use in me pretending that it is someone else who has captured my attention when they have not." She glanced back toward his lordship, and

Wes narrowed his eyes at the small, devilish smile that lifted her lips.

Did she truly want Lord Poulett? "So your interest lies with the marquess?" he scoffed and couldn't hide the sarcasm in his response. "I would have thought Lord Abercromby at least over Poulett. Do you not think he is a little soft about the edges to be your husband? And do not forget he lives in the wilds of Cornwall. You will never be seen again should you marry him."

He met Harlow's eyes and could see multiple questions blaze within her green depths. Questions that he, too, had been asking himself and could not answer. Questions with answers he did not want to face or admit.

And certainly not now.

Harlow watched Lord Kemsley and fought to school her features at the thinly veiled jealousy that masked every look and drop of information he made at her side.

She supposed it would be hard for a rake to admit when they liked another, certainly when they did not wish to. And she knew to the very core of her soul that Kemsley was a rogue and enjoyed that lifestyle very much. In fact, he was famous for it since arriving in London at the age of eighteen.

But then, he had never thought of meeting a

woman like herself, and she liked that she offered a new path to walk. Perhaps not one he wished for, but one he could not live without if he fell in love with her.

If he wanted to marry her.

He desired her, that was certain, but she needed to make him choose, and that in itself was not as easy as making him flustered and bothered by her nearness.

"I think his softness will soon turn to hardness when I need it to," she taunted, hoping he understood that her words did not mean anything naïve.

His shocked countenance told her he did. He adjusted his cravat. His swallow was almost audible. "What will you do with him? What is your plan?"

She bit her lip, hiding her grin. Was his voice a little too strained? "I thought I may ask to go for a walk with his lordship, discuss matters which we both find interesting, and touch his lordship. Here or there," she said, reaching out and touching Kemsley's arm, sliding her hand down his superfine coat before taking his hand. She held it but a moment before dropping it. "What do you think?" she asked him.

He cleared his throat. "I think that will work well, but what next? I do not think holding his hand will make him bend at the knee and offer marriage."

Harlow stepped closer to Kemsley. He stood beside a tree, and with her behind him, he relatively hid her from the view of the ball. "I could touch him here." She reached out and placed her hand on his hip, his coat hiding her touch. Harlow tightened her hold, the muscles beneath her fingers flexing. "I could pull him close, like this," she said, pulling Kemsley toward her. "Look up at his lordship, let him see that I want him, tonight and always, see if he understands my plea and kisses me."

Her body was not itself. Her skin prickled. Her stomach twisted and turned with delicious need. She watched Kemsley, saw the echoing desire in his blue eyes, and wanted to shout, "Kiss me, you fool."

"I think," he said, stepping closer to her and moving them farther into the shadowy garden, "that you are well-versed in the art of seduction and no longer need my instruction."

Panic assailed her, and her mind whirred with what to say. How to amend his thinking. "Come, my lord." She chuckled. "There is much more to learn. Surely you have not shown me everything."

His eyes darkened further. Another step against her, pushing them out of view of others. "To teach you more would be ruination, Harlow," he said, using her given name for the first time. "Is that what you want?"

She shivered, watched him, saw the question,

the plea in his eyes. She understood that question, for she too held the same. She wanted what he offered, all of it, so long as she could prolong having him in her arms.

"Yes, it is what I want," she admitted, just before he seized her face in his hands and kissed her.

Hard.

Sixteen

Harlow wrapped her arms around his neck and kissed him back. She threw all that she had learned, all she felt and wanted, into the kiss that left her reeling.

He picked her up, his arms linked beneath her bottom, and walked them farther into the dark park. Only when the music was a muted echo through the shrubbery and garden beds did he slip her down to her feet.

For a moment, she thought he might change his mind, turn on his heel and leave her wanting him with such a fierce need that she knew no matter who saw them, she would go after him and demand he finish what he started.

Instead, he took her lips for a second time. Their tongues tangled for seniority, hands were everywhere, not just Kemsley's. His body was like steel beneath her fingers, his breathing ragged, his stomach hard, his chest rising in quick succession.

He sat on a nearby stone seat and pulled her onto his lap. But this was no innocent way of sitting on another's knees. He had her straddle him.

"Shuffle up your dress. It'll make sitting on me easier," his gravelly voice demanded.

She did as he asked. Never in her life had she felt so exposed. Not even when they were alone on her lawn this afternoon. Somehow, with her legs spread and placed so close to his manhood, this felt far more intimate.

And she adored it.

"What now?" she invited, adjusting her seat to slip her arms around his neck a second time, bringing her mons closer to his groin.

He reached between them, and she heard the buttons holding his falls closed popping. "Your turn to learn how to touch me," he instructed, taking one of her hands and edging it between them.

Harlow needed no further prompting. She moved her dress out of the way and found his phallus, hard and erect, jutting between them. She gasped, slipping her fingers around his bulging length, so silky soft yet hard and determined.

"I did not know you would feel like this," she said, unable to hide the awe in her tone.

"Stroke me with your hand," he instructed.

"Like this." He covered her hand with his, squeezing it a little before moving up and down. His eyes met hers, and she read the need that burned like wildfire.

"You like this?" she asked, knowing he did.

"Yes," he breathed, stealing a kiss, one that Harlow pushed further. She needed to taste him, have him in all ways.

Their tongues echoed what her touch did on his manhood, and he groaned, pulling her close.

"How far would you like me to teach you, Harlow?" he asked her. He removed her hand, slipping it over his shoulder before pulling her against his manhood.

The velvety hardness pressed against her cunny, and exquisite delight thrummed through her. He guided her against him, up and down, and Harlow lost all coherent thought.

"As far as one can go," she answered, never wanting to remove herself from his lap. He felt so good. A teasing, taunting tool that made her body thrum in the most delectable way. "Show me everything."

WES KNEW HE COULD NOT SHOW HER everything, but damn it all to hell, he would enjoy what he could show her this evening, even if it were only a taste of what they could relish.

"The things I could show you, Harlow.

You're a passionate woman, and you would enjoy everything," he said, taking her lips, relishing her taste and the feel of her tongue sliding against his. Her warm, welcoming body that fit him like a kid leather glove.

She was a fast learner, and there was no turning back from what they had started this evening. Nor did he wish to. He had to have her. Be her first.

As selfish as that thought was, she was his tonight, and no one, not even Lord Poulett, would take that from him.

Not that he could solely blame himself for his rakish wiles. Harlow had sought him out and had asked for further instruction, and he could not refuse her wishes. What type of gentleman would he be to deny a lady what she wanted?

He would be no gentleman at all.

He guided her up, lifting her to kneel before running his cock between her wet folds. So hot and moist, a ready and willing cunny if ever there was one.

"Lower yourself onto me," he stated.

She nodded, and he held himself still as she guided herself down upon him. He bit the inside of his lip as, with glorious slowness, she took his length.

So tight, hot, and wet. Never had he ever had the overwhelming urge to cherish this moment, to remember it always and keep it safe in his heart.

"Are you well, Harlow?" he asked her when she settled upon him, not moving.

Her eyes widened, and she met his gaze. "I feel ... I feel wonderful. What do I do now?" she asked him, eager as always.

He breathed a sigh of relief before wrapping his arms firmly about her. She was perfection in his arms, and he adored having her just so. "Lift yourself up and down on me. Similar to what you did with your hand, except now we are joined in truth, wholly and without fail."

She nodded, doing as he asked, as tentative and torturous as her slowness was. She used her knees, moving on him, and he fought to control his base desires. His need to control the situation, to lift her and take her with more determined strokes, almost overrode his patience.

This she had to do at her own pace and in her own time. If he wanted to be with her again just so, he could not scare her. Not that there should be a second time, but now that he had her, he was certain that once would never be enough.

He doubted that even twice would be enough.

Mayhap three times would satisfy the craving she initiated within him.

"How is this?" she asked.

"So good," he growled, helping her fall into a

rhythm, a dance that swept him away and one he never wished would end.

AT FIRST, HARLOW COULD NOT HELP BUT regret her decision this evening. Being with Wes as they are now, making love to him was not the most comfortable thing to do. But the more she joined with him, his large, strong hands guiding her, not pushing her, his wicked kisses that stole her breath and heart soon brought a warmth to replace the stinging pain, and she grew to enjoy what they were doing more and more.

He was large and filled her completely. She closed her eyes, rocking against him. When she had come to the ball this evening, she had hoped for more instruction, kisses, and teasing as they had partaken these past weeks.

She had not expected this, but now that she was with him, she would never want to be with anyone else.

"You feel so good," she admitted, taking his lips.

He kissed her hard, stealing her breath. "I would lay you on the grass and make love to you if I could, Harlow, but your gown would be ruined, and so too your reputation if I did," he teased.

She chuckled, gasping when he pushed into

her, taking her with a little more force than before.

"Mmm, I like that, my lord. Do not stop," she begged of him.

His eyes darkened with wicked intent, his fingers firmer against her hips. "Like this?" he asked her, thrusting into her again.

"Yes," she breathed, the need that thrummed within her unlike anything she had ever experienced. "Touch me, please," she begged, not sure why exactly, but some inner voice told her that was what she needed.

He did as she asked without delay, slipping his hand between them to roll his fingers against her sex. Exquisite pleasure pulsed when his hand teased, and she looked up to the stars, certain she was floating with them right at this moment.

"Come for me, Harlow," he demanded, rolling her sex, his clever fingers taunting her as he had before. "I want to hear my name on your lips," he stated, his breath mingling with hers.

Her pace increased, and she rode him with more vigor. She was so full, her sex aching and thrumming with desire. She was so close she could feel herself on the precipice of something wonderful.

If only she could reach it.

He thrust into her several times, his fingers flicking her sex with perfect timing, and she catapulted into a sea of bliss. Her body convulsed with her release. Wes muffled her moan with a kiss as her body thrummed and echoed with ecstasy, unlike anything she had ever known.

"Wes," she moaned, clasping his jaw with her hands. "What about you? I cannot be the only one who enjoys such delights this evening."

He chuckled, shaking his head. "It is best that I do not go any further, but I promise you, there are other ways a man can spend."

"Really?" she asked, curious. "How?"

His unscrupulous grin almost made her shatter once more. "Let me explain."

Seventeen

The sound of voices interrupted their solitude, and Wes quickly repaired Harlow's attire and inspected her hair to ensure all was as it should be before he sent her back to the ball through the gardens in a way she would not be seen.

He watched her reenter the supper box her family had procured for the evening but stayed in the gardens for several minutes, gaining his equilibrium.

He had fucked a maid, practically a debutante, and a woman who was related to his friend, and a best friend to several families of status.

He ought to offer her marriage. But she did not want him in that way. Yes, she had enjoyed the tup they had partaken in, but that did not mean anything.

She had not changed her mind about the

lessons and, in fact, thought what they had done was all part of his schooling.

He ground his teeth, giving his attire one last check before returning to the outdoor ball. A footman passed him, and he took a glass of brandy, downing it without thought.

What if she married Lord Poulett but had his child growing in her belly? He swallowed the bile that rose in his throat, and for the first time since starting these lessons, his thoughts did not sit well on his conscience.

She stood not far from him, sipping wine and talking to the Marchioness of Chilsten. Her gaze lighted on him several times, her skin flushed from their escapades, her lips swollen from his kisses.

His body thrummed, knowing that there was another part of her that would be swollen and aching from his touch. A small, knowing smile lifted her lips, and he fought not to wrench her back out into the several dark walks and have her a second time.

Several minutes passed before she joined him at the side of the outdoor ballroom floor, looking at him expectantly. "Are you going to tell me how else I can please a gentleman, my lord? You've already taught me so much this evening, and you did mention you would," she said, her eyes wide and mischievous.

He inwardly groaned, unsure if speaking of

what she wanted was a good idea, but then, when had he thought clearly when around Harlow York? Whenever had he done anything resembling common sense?

"Are you sure you wish to know? You may become embarrassed, and people may speculate about what we're talking about. It may damage your progress with Lord Poulett."

Her mouth pursed into a displeased line, and he was glad she took his warning seriously.

"Even so, I wish to know. If I have any chance of winning my intended, I need to know everything as we agreed when we started these lessons," she replied, watching him keenly.

He stared at her a moment, drinking in her beauty and wondering why it had taken him so long to notice she was one of the most handsome women of his acquaintance. It was no wonder she had been named the Season's diamond last year.

"Very well, but I shall be frank without embellishments. Those elaborations you will have to learn yourself when you're married. I would suggest not partaking in this before taking your vows."

She nodded. "Understood and intrigued," she said.

Wes cleared his throat, looking about to ensure they were reasonably alone. "A man may free himself from his breeches, and a woman may take him into her mouth, lick and suck on his appendage as if it were a sweet until he finds his release."

Her mouth gaped before she licked her lips in an enticing way. "Is that not difficult for the woman?" she queried, biting her bottom lip. He inwardly groaned, wanting those lips on him and not just on his mouth. Why were they talking about this? It was not safe, nor was it appropriate.

"Depends on how large the man is," he answered without thinking. Her eyes widened, and curiosity sparkled in her green depths.

"Does size matter, my lord?" She stepped closer, and he felt the brush of her hand on his leg. "What would a woman say about you, Lord Kemsley? What would you term your size as?" she asked without chagrin.

It was his turn to gape at her, and for a moment, he could not form a reply. The chit had gumption and knew very well what his size was. In time she would come to learn that this conversation was in no way respectable or should be taking place.

Not that it stopped him from continuing it.

"I'm proportionate to my height and know what to do with myself to ensure a lady's enjoyment," he answered, not willing to blow his own horn over his appendage, not that he hadn't been told it was quite formidable and capable when up to the task.

HARLOW BIT BACK A GRIN. SHE WAS teasing him, prodding him to answer her, not that he seemed willing to tell her outright that his manhood was more than satisfactory. And it had satisfied her more quickly than she thought it could, given it was her first time with a man.

That he would be the only man she ever slept with was what she needed to work on now. "Proportionate? Hmm, well, I'm no expert, but I would say that I was filled quite satisfactorily by you, and each time we, well, you know," she said, meeting his eye. "Each time I moved in a downward motion, I found you teased something within me, a button of some sort if I should give it a name that made me feel so wonderful." She sighed, remembering their joining. "And then, as for the conclusion of our meeting, well, that was bewitching."

His eyes blazed down on her, and he shifted on his feet before looking out at the entertained multitude of guests. "You will feel the same with your intended, and now you know what to expect."

Harlow inwardly growled, wanting to scream at the blind man. Did he truly think she would give herself to him only to learn a lesson? She could not believe, would not think that he thought so lowly of her to consider that. Tonight she had placed herself at risk, and he could not think she would do that without affection of some kind.

Lord Kemsley had to be protecting himself and his heart.

He did not finish in you. In fact, he did not find release at all, so there is no risk ... is there?

"I think I shall find Lord Poulett," she said. "Mayhap, I can persuade him to stroll the gardens, and I can put what I have learned this evening and all our other nights together into practice," she said, calling his bluff.

Harlow strolled from his side, moving through the crowd of people, but not to find Lord Poulett as she had threatened. Instead, she strolled toward the Necessary House that accommodated the retiring room, needing to compose herself.

Kemsley could not have made love to her and now thought she was well enough to do it with another man. He could not be such a cad. She proceeded to the three-story building at the edge of the gardens and went inside. A maid at the door directed her to where the retiring room was, and just as she moved past the stairs, a hand came about her back, pulling her hard against his person.

Before Harlow could utter a word of protest,

she was shoved into a little storage room under the stairs, the barest of light from the foyer their only means to see.

"You would fuck Poulett after what we just did?" Kemsley's words sounded ripped and shredded, and she backed away from him, unsure of his disposition.

"That is what your lessons are for, are they not?" she stated, needing him to answer, to realize that maybe just the smallest part of himself was jealous of that fact and ought to do something about it.

"Tonight, you're mine," he said instead before his lips crashed down on hers. She gasped, clinging to him. Need and anger smothered every touch, every kiss.

He kneeled before her, his hot mouth, his tongue, tickling the inside of her knee.

"I forgot to mention that a man can pleasure a woman in the same way I mentioned before," he said, throwing up her skirts.

His mouth worked its way up her legs, paying homage to both thighs, teasing the sensitive skin of her inner thighs before he lifted one of her legs, settling it over his shoulder.

Harlow reached out, holding on to the underside of the stairs, hoping her legs would not collapse under the onslaught of his mouth. He licked her cunny, sending light to blaze before her eyes. His mouth kissed her as if he were kissing her lips, suckling, taunting, pushing her toward the peak she needed again, craved like air.

With one hand, she clasped his head, unable to stop undulating against his mouth, which worked its wicked magic on her sex.

Heat licked her skin, and she bit her lip, fighting to stop the moan she wanted to scream and shout to the world as his mouth took her in a way she had never thought possible.

She closed her eyes, gave herself up to the pleasure, and then it rolled through her, ache after delicious ache, tremor after delicious tremor, while his mouth milked her to the very end of her pleasure.

Harlow clung to him, limp, and fought not to slump into a puddle of exquisite satisfaction.

"Wes," she whispered, waiting as he came to stand before her. She could barely make out his face, all hard angles and eyes blazing with need.

"Harlow," he whispered back before his mouth took hers, but this kiss was different. Soft and long, a waltz of seduction that was an unhurried and sweet dance.

She kissed him, reaching up to hold him close, to keep him near, now and forever. Her heart was his, and she prayed he would give his to her in return.

Eighteen

Wes felt the tug against his superfine coat and turned to find the displeased visage of his good friend Lord Howley. He raised his brow, wondering why Howley did not greet him. "Is something the matter?" he asked the earl, the pit of his gut churning at the disapproval in his friend's eyes, putting him on edge.

"Yes, there are a few things, one of which is that I viewed you yesterday shuffling Miss York into the cupboard under the stairs in the Necessary House. I can only assume you had some important tidbit to discuss with the young unmarried miss because I'm certain that you would not have escorted her there for any other reason."

Wes felt the blood drain from his face, and he fought not to choke on his brandy. He had been seen? "Did anyone else see?" he asked one of his oldest friends.

"No," Howley said, his eyes narrowing. "But that does not make it right or an action that does not come without some sort of consequence."

"It is not what you think," he explained, knowing that for the lie it was. "I'm helping Miss York learn the art of seduction so she may use it against the gentleman she does wish to marry. Believe me, it is not I that she wants. I'm merely the vessel that will enable her match to be a happy and passionate one."

Howley raised a skeptical brow and stared at him as if Wes had sprouted two heads.

"I know you do not believe me, but you must swear you will say nothing. She does not wish for me to be her husband, and all her hard work will be for naught if you make us marry."

"She looked well-satisfied when you left the safety of that staircase cupboard. What types of teachings are you giving her?" Howley asked him.

Wes waved his question aside. No way in heaven was he going to tell him what he had done to Harlow under those stairs. The memory made heat lick at his skin. Worse, what he had done to her was not the most flawed of it. He had taken her as a man should be able to take his wife. Howley would demand marriage if he knew that truth.

"The way to look at her intended, speak, give

subtle gestures on how to raise his awareness of her. Innocent things like that," he lied.

His friend looked far from impressed by his explanation. "I have kept many secrets for you over the years before your marriage to the Woodville chit. You owe me, Howley," Wes stated, willing to use that card in his pocket if only to keep his friend from making him marry a woman he did not want as his wife.

He supposed if he were to marry anyone, Harlow would be adequate, and he was sure they would rub along nicely together, but that was not what she wanted.

Not what he wanted.

He was a free man. A rake and a man who enjoyed the company of many, not one.

He caught sight of Harlow as she floated about the dance floor within the arms of Lord Poulett. The gentleman she did wish to marry.

"See," Wes said, gesturing to Harlow. "Miss York is happier with Lord Poulett. Do not ruin all her plans merely because I'm being helpful to an innocent lady who did not know how to go about winning the love of the man she desired."

Howley stared at Miss York, his eyes narrowing in thought. Wes prayed he would believe his true words.

Well ... almost true.

He watched Harlow. He reveled in the sight of her in her pink empire-style gown that accentuated her breasts. Breasts that were plump and reactive to his touch. Her fair skin, the color of alabaster, unmarked, that smelled so damn good that even now he was sure he could smell roses.

But above all of her outward beauty was her inner loveliness. She was witty, smart, kind, and passionate, everything a man ought to want in a wife.

What he ought to want.

"She appears to be enjoying herself, but something is missing. There is no spark, and speaking from a man who knows what it is to live with a woman who sparks to life in your arms, let me tell you, Kemsley, Miss York does not have it with Lord Poulett." He paused, clapping him on the shoulder. "But when she left the staircase cupboard yesterday evening, by God, she sparkled like a rare jewel, and you caused that. Not anyone else," his friend stated before throwing him a knowing smile and leaving him to mull over his words.

Wes swallowed the panic that assailed him, along with pride. Had he made her sparkle? His lips twitched before he schooled his features. What was he doing? He did not care if she sparkled at all. She did not want him. She wanted Lord Poulett.

He did not want a wife. His married brother had a son; marriage was not a priority.

Wes took a deep breath, and the first lady

who crossed his path he asked to dance, anything but to think over Howley's words. The young lady accepted with more excitement than he felt was warranted for a minuet. He pulled her into line, linking arms and partaking in idle chat as the dance progressed, but still, his mind would not calm.

Did Harlow want him over Lord Poulett?

He caught sight of her on the side of the ballroom floor through the multitude of steps of the dance, and his question was answered. Her lips were pursed tight in a displeased line, her eyes narrowed in annoyance, and realization struck.

She may have wished for Lord Poulett at first, but she also was not immune to feeling jealousy when he was paying court to someone else.

Did that mean she had changed her mind? That, he did not know, nor would he ask.

Liar. The thought of her marrying any man makes you sick to your stomach.

He ignored his warning, throwing himself into the dance, even bestowing Miss Somersea a teasing grin or two. He would not succumb to the marriage state as so many of his friends had. Nor would he make a good husband. He would be bored within a week.

Liar. His mind taunted again. *Not with Harlow, you would not.*

And this time, he knew that statement to be true. Something told him to be married to

Harlow would be different, not monotonous or stale. If anything, it would be the opposite.

Probably bloody marvelous in truth.

HARLOW WOULD NO LONGER TORTURE herself watching Wes as he danced first with Miss Somersea, then a gaggle of young women, many of whom seemed far too in awe of his lordship for the good of his vanity.

She did not need him thinking more highly of himself than he already did. He was a rogue, aware of his allure to the opposite sex. Should he consider himself a martyr to the opposite sex, there would be no stopping him.

And in any case, he was hers. Not any of the other young ladies who took his hand. She stood on the side of the ballroom floor, wondering when he would bow before her and ask her to dance.

That he had not sent a cold shiver down her spine.

What game was he playing? Was he trying to teach her a lesson? Prove to himself that he did not care for her? He did. To her very core, she knew that he did, so to make out otherwise was foolish of him.

"Miss York, a glass of lemonade just as you requested," Lord Poulett proclaimed at her side, handing her a small glass.

"Thank you," she said, taking a sip. "That is most refreshing." She bestowed his lordship a pleased smile and then turned back to watch the guests. Well, one guest in particular, who looked too striking for his own good.

"Now that we're alone and have a moment to talk privately, there is something that I wished to discuss with you if you're willing to speak to me now on the matter," Lord Poulett stated.

Harlow studied his lordship and noted the slight sheen of sweat on his upper lip. She turned and gave him her full attention. "Of course, my lord. You may tell me what is bothering you," she answered.

He smiled, clearing his throat. "Nothing is bothering me, Miss York. That is to say, nothing is bothering me yet, but should you answer my question to the opposite of which I would like you to, then I may feel a little discomfort after the fact."

A little discomfort? No more than what she was feeling right at this moment. The urge to flee rode hard on her heels, but she remained, did her duty as a well-bred young lady ought, and hear out a gentleman when they had something to say. "What is your question, my lord?"

He lifted his chin, steeling himself to speak. "My question is whether you would consider being my wife." He took her hand, lifting it to his lips. "Will you marry me, Miss York?"

Startled gasps sounded about her, along with several claps from people who were listening in. The room spun. Harlow had hoped that this question would never be asked of her, unless it was by Lord Kemsley.

She glanced around the room and noted the bright, eager gazes and large, joyous smiles at his lordship's public proposal. She might add that it was far louder than she had thought it should have been.

Harlow swallowed the bile that rose in her throat, and her heart stopped at the sight of Lord Kemsley, standing in the middle of the ballroom floor, his dance partner idle beside him, confusion written on her pretty face at his lordship's abrupt halt to their *Allemande*.

Without trying to stop her answer, Lord Kemsley turned on his heel and left, leaving her to face Lord Poulett and to answer his question before all the *ton*.

Nineteen

"Lord Poulett," Harlow's brother-in-law Lord Billington said, coming up to her side. "Perhaps we can discuss such matters in my office tomorrow at noon. Tonight's entertainment is not the appropriate time, I feel." He took her arm, slipping it about his.

Her sister, Lady Billington, joined her husband, standing on the other side of Harlow, cushioning her from any further requests of marriage or whatever other questions may come her way.

Harlow glanced up at them both. Lord Billington looked less than pleased, her sister's expression full of compassion for Lord Poulett.

"Of course," Lord Poulett said, bowing. "I do apologize for making my desires known. I shall call on you tomorrow to discuss the matter."

"Very good," Billington said. "Good evening."

Within a few minutes, Harlow was whisked from the ball and soon found herself ensconced in the viscount's carriage, her sister and brother-in-law seated across from her, quiet in their musings.

"Are you mad at me?" Harlow asked, trying to figure out exactly what was happening between them.

"No, not at all, but I do not appreciate Lord Poulett asking for your hand at the ball after I had informed him to call on us tomorrow only an hour before. I feel he went against my word and tried to force your hand before the *ton*. Not an act of a gentleman at all."

He had asked Billington for her hand earlier? She had not known that tidbit.

"Do you know, sister, that he has a mistress he has stated publicly at Whites that he means to keep? For all his wealth and castle in Cornwall, I would not let you marry the cad even if he asked in the privacy of our home."

"Lila, I told you that in confidence," Billington chided.

Her sister shrugged, patting her husband's knee as if to appease him. "When such matters may influence my sister's choice and happiness in life, I shall always tell her what I know," she said. "That you told me this information is one of the reasons why I married you, darling. You do not keep secrets from me."

Harlow smiled and glanced out the window. "So he wanted to force my hand." Well, that had not worked. "I suppose tomorrow we shall have to tell him that his suit is not welcome." Harlow chewed her bottom lip, wondering what she would do now.

For weeks she had taunted Lord Kemsley that she wanted Lord Poulett, or one of the other men who had taken a keen interest in her to marry her. Had led Kemsley to believe that it was Lord Poulett that she wanted as her husband above any of the others.

If she said no tomorrow, which she had every intention of doing, Kemsley would know that she had been lying to him for weeks. He would, of course, wonder what her inclination was the entire time.

He would discover that, in truth, she wanted him and no one else, and he would feel like she played him the fool.

She worked her hands in her lap, her mind frantically trying to think of a way to clear a path forward for her. She had hoped by now Kemsley would have realized he was in love with her and would offer his hand in marriage.

"I think you should answer no," Lila said. "He would not make you happy, I do not believe."

Harlow could believe that very well. Kemsley had told her of Poulett's Cornwall estate and wealth, but he had failed to mention the mistress. Maybe he did not know as much as Billington did of the gentleman. But then, her sister and

Billington were acting as her guardians this year, and that position meant they needed to know all about her suitors.

The carriage rolled to a halt before the Georgian town house, and Harlow followed her sister and brother-in-law indoors.

"Would you like a cup of tea in the library before we retire?" Lila asked her.

She shook her head, no longer in the mood for any company. What she needed now was quiet and time alone. To think and plan and decide how to let Poulett down nicely and explain how she would tell Kemsley why she had.

"No, I think I shall bid you both goodnight. I'm very tired," she said, her slippered feet uncomfortably heavy along with her eyelids.

"Goodnight then, sister," Lila said.

"Goodnight," Harlow replied, starting upstairs. Thankfully her maid was waiting for her, and she endured the taking down of her hair, the many pins that required moving, along with her dress, stays, and stockings that followed.

Before long she was tucked up in bed, candles snuffed, and alone at last. Just as she needed to be to think straight and plan.

It did not take Wes long to climb the trellis to the second floor of Billington's town house. The hardest part was ensuring he was not caught before he found Harlow's bedroom.

This evening the air was sticky and warm in London, and thankfully several upstairs windows were cracked open just the smallest bit to allow any breeze that may rise. That a trellis sat beneath one window in particular was providential. He really ought to tell Billington before someone willing to do the family harm caught on and stole from them, or worse.

Not that he was innocent in his breaking and entering the London town house. He needed to see Harlow. Talk to her, ask her if she had answered Lord Poulett, which he had not stayed around to find out.

He ground his teeth, ignoring the few jabs from the jasmine vine as he climbed and tried to forget how the ballroom had spun the moment Lord Poulett had proposed to Harlow before all the *ton*.

Was the man mad? Who proposed in the middle of a ball? The very idea made his blood run cold.

Worse was he had not stayed to find out if she said yes.

Tomorrow was too far away to discover the answer, and so he continued to climb, needing to know and to persuade her to rethink her choice if she had said yes.

Lord Poulett was not for her. Why she

thought he was above anyone else that courted her this year, he could not fathom. Not to mention he had tried numerous times to dissuade him. He was a cad, not loyal or capable of loving one woman. In truth, he was no better than Lord Hill. He would break her heart, and Harlow was his friend. He would not see her hurt.

His teaching here may have started as innocent fun, a way to pass London's boring Season, but it had long strayed from such mediocrity. He looked forward to seeing her. Teaching her the ways to win a man's heart, but he also looked forward to talking to her.

She had become one of his closest friends, and if she became betrothed now, that would all change. They would no longer be able to spend time together and converse as they once had.

He was not ready to give her over to anyone yet, and certainly not Lord Poulett.

Reaching the first floor, he pushed the window open farther and hoisted himself inside. The room was spacious. A large bed took up most of the space. The fire was a dark shadow, and he could just make out a person who slept in the bed.

With the greatest care, he edged his way over to the bed, moving out of the moonlight piercing the room, and sighed in relief that he had managed to climb into Harlow's room and not Lord and Lady Billington's.

"Harlow," he whispered, kneeling beside her. "Harlow, it's me, Wes," he whispered again. Should he cover her mouth to stop her from startling and screaming awake? If he were caught here, there would be no stopping them from marrying, no matter how much they both did not want it.

A little voice in his mind scoffed at his thoughts, and he ignored them. "Harlow," he tried again. "Please do not scream. It's only me. Wes," he tried again.

She stirred and made a delicious little mewling sound that sent heat straight to his groin before a small frown kissed her brow. "Hmm, what?" she mumbled.

"Harlow, it's me. Wes. Please wake up, but don't scream," he reminded her.

Her frown deepened, and her eyes fluttered before she gasped, scooting back in the bed to come up hard against the bedhead. "What is ..." She paused, blinked, and he saw the moment she comprehended who was in her room.

"Kemsley?" she asked, peering at him. "What are you doing here?" she whispered ferociously, glancing at the door. "You cannot be in here. What if you're caught?"

"We would be married, but I had to know. I could not sleep with what had been plaguing my mind."

She sat forward, patting the bed. He stood

and sat beside her. "What do you mean? Why are you worried, my lord?" she asked him.

He clasped her jaw, tipping up her chin so he could easily see into her green depths. "Tell me did you agree to marry Lord Poulett? Tell me that you did not."

A puzzled expression crossed her pretty features before she shook her head. Relief, sweet and satisfying, ran through him at her answer. "No, I did not reply to his lordship. Billington asked him to call on us tomorrow to discuss the matter, but my sister is against the match. Lord Poulett is apparently quite taken with his mistress, whom he does not want to remove from his life after taking a bride, and I will not abide sharing my husband, whomever that may be, with any other woman."

"Did I not tell you he was not worthy of you? There are others who are. Good men who would make a good husband."

Like you ...

Good God, what was he thinking? He did not want to marry. Did not want marriage at all at his age.

Did he?

If he did not marry Harlow, then she would marry one day, mayhap not this month or the next, but eventually, she would find a man she loved, and she would marry. Be lost to him forever.

She nodded, her eyes sparkling in the moonlight like gems. "You did say that to me. I'm so thankful for your friendship and guidance."

"You will always have it," he said, dipping his head and kissing her quickly.

A small smile lifted her lips, her hands curling about the lapels of his coat. "What was that for?" she asked him. "Are we having another lesson?"

He shook his head. "No lessons, Harlow. Not tonight. For one night, I'm just a man sitting on a woman's bed that I desire, asking her to be with me. No lessons. No tutorials. No questions asked." He kissed her again, longer this time. "Just us, until the breaking dawn."

"Is this not against your rules, Kemsley? A little too intimate. What if you grow feelings for me? Whatever shall you do?" she teased him.

He chuckled, moving his hands to untie the small ribbons that held her shift closed at her neck. "I will not. Your future is safe out of my hands," he admitted, wondering why the words left a hollow pit in his chest, a gaping crevice that wept like an open wound. "But tonight, you are all mine."

THE WORD *MINE* REVERBERATED IN Harlow's mind, and she wanted to scream to the world that he was hers too. All hers and no one else's.

Was his being here the start of his growing feelings toward her? Was he jealous?

Harlow threw herself into his arms, wanting to be with him again with a need that left her breathless and impatient. He swept her off the bed and onto his lap before lying down upon her mattress, coming over her, and pressing her down into the many blankets.

She reached for him, held him close, and threw herself into the kiss. Their tongues tangled and fought for dominance. He tasted of whisky, of wickedness, and future-husband material.

He would be hers.

Ask me she wanted to shout.

His hands worked fast on her shift. Cool air kissed her legs before he swept it over her head, throwing it somewhere in the room along with any innocence she had left.

Not that she did. She had already been with Kemsley, and now he was here, stealing into her room in the middle of the night to make love to her.

"Help me undress. I want your hands on me," he told her.

Harlow would do whatever he wished. She untied his cravat and pushed off his coat, needing to feel him better.

For a moment, she reveled in his muscular chest, his taut stomach. "I like how you feel." She held her hand against his heart. "Your heart is beating fast."

He grinned, ripping his shirt over his head before taking her hand and placing it back on his body. "I like you touching me too," he admitted to her.

This had to be love. He must be feeling more for her than mere friendship. This could not be how he was with all his past lovers. Harlow could not believe that callousness of him. He was better than that.

"I also wanted to be with you in a bed. You deserve to be loved on a bed of silk, cushions at your back, and every luxury afforded to you."

"Will you feed me grapes should I demand you to?" she asked teasingly.

He chuckled, nodding. "Of course."

She reached down and flicked the few buttons about his silk, knee-high breeches before untying them fully.

He sat up, leaving her bereft before he kicked off his pants.

Harlow's eyes grew wide at the sight of him standing before her, naked as the day he was born, hungry and hard, his determined eyes pinned decidedly on her.

A shiver stole over her body, and her heart kicked up a beat. Wetness pooled at her core, and never had she wanted a man as much as she wanted Kemsley.

Wes...

She reached for him, and he came down upon her, settling between her legs. His manhood pressed against her core, and she sought him, needed him with a hunger that surpassed sensibility.

He thrust into her, making them one. One strong arm clasped her thigh, lifting it high on his hip, and she moaned. He stretched her, filled her, made her whole.

So good. So maddening.

"Wes," she moaned, and he growled, taking her lips in a kiss that left her breathless, unable to think. She lost herself in his arms, his body working hers, pushing her toward the peak she wanted to reach.

Desperately.

With relentlessness and stamina that she had not thought possible, he made love to her, kissed her, and seduced her even more to be his. Now and forever.

"Harlow," he whispered against her lips. "Tell me you will not marry Poulett."

She met his eyes and saw the fear that lurked in his blue depths. "I will not marry him. You have my word. I couldn't. Not when I ..." She bit her lip, scoring his back with her fingernails when he thrust harder, deeper, taunting her more.

"When you what?" he asked, watching her, his eyes ablaze.

"He is not who I want. Not really," she said but was unable to say more. But she would. Tomorrow she would request to see him. It was time to tell him the truth, make him choose.

Please choose me.

"He is not good enough for you," he whispered against her lips. Harlow gasped when he rolled onto his back. She followed him, coming to sit on top of him.

Her fingers splayed against his chest, and this way, she could better see his magnificence. Not to mention he went deeper, the sensation more fulfilling.

Harlow shifted and sampled how this new position felt before lifting herself. She moaned as frissons of pleasure passed through her body.

His hands reached up, cupping her breasts, a wicked lift to his lips. "You're so beautiful, Harlow. You undo me," he said.

Harlow leaned down and kissed him, welcomed his arms that came about her back and held her. Full with love, with Wes, and that was enough to shatter her into millions of pieces.

He kissed her through her release, muffling her scream before following her into their bliss, linking them together and, with any deity intervention, forever.

TWENTY

The next few weeks of the Season were days of longing filled with nights of incandescent bliss and some very, very naughty antics.

Harlow had not thought she would be so exceedingly bad, but when it came to Wes, she found that she could be the worst of ladies. With merely a look, a glance across the room, she was lost.

A flick of his head and she would go with him, meet him, be alone with him.

However would she part from him should he not declare himself? But she was certain he would and very soon. They were spending so much time together, and not only when they were being intimate, although that did take up quite a few hours of every night.

That Lord Poulett had not taken her refusal of him well, and consistently tried to change her mind, also helped. She had not had to try to explain why she had needed the lessons from Wes, and nor had she gained enough nerve to tell him how she felt.

But his lessons had changed now, and they had morphed into need between the two of them. Harlow understood what that need meant for her in any case. She was in love with Wes.

But did he love her? Had he reconciled that his bachelorhood was ending, and she was the woman for him? That she could not say, but it did not stop her from convincing him otherwise.

To walk with her down the aisle.

Tonight was the Devonshire ball. Everyone who was anyone was invited. Already Harlow had spoken to the Woodville girls, now all happily married, and her sister, who had chaperoned her here over the magnificent ballroom, the gilded mirrors, and marble fireplaces.

Wes was still to arrive, but she knew he would be here soon. He had promised her that he would attend and dance with her twice.

A small smile lifted her lips at the thought of him. The idea that after all they had been through, all the things they had done together that he would still walk away left a knot in her stomach.

A hand brushed the nape of her neck before whispered words brushed her ear. "Good evening," he said, coming to stand at her side.

Harlow shivered at his touch, and he threw her a wicked grin that promised all the delights he bestowed on her most evenings.

"Lord Kemsley. A little tardy this evening, are you not? I thought I may be forced to dance with Lord Hill, who circles as we speak."

"I would never allow such a travesty," he said, smiling at her and making her catch her breath. He was so handsome. To be near him made her want to sigh at the delight of his looks.

Not to mention they got along very well in other aspects too.

"I hope you have come prepared to dance. I believe there is a country dance up soon. A lively jig that should be entertaining."

"I shall be all yours." He held out his arm, and she wrapped her hand about him. His muscles flexed under his superfine coat, and she reveled in the feel of him. How she had missed him since last night when he had snuck into her bedroom window yet again.

They had started to sleep together quite often, but last night had been different. Last night they had slept, had held each other, and nothing more. To be with Wes in such a way had to mean he was in love with her as much as she loved him.

There was no other explanation.

The orchestra started to play the first notes of the country dance, and with a squeal of delight, Wes pulled her out onto the floor to join the other couples. The dance lasted for several minutes. They danced, laughed, spoke to other guests, and never had she enjoyed herself so much with anyone.

How could he not want this forever?

"Your cheeks are flushed quite prettily," he said when they were skipping between other couples. "Seeing you like this, happy, smiling, your green eyes alight with life and fire makes me want to kiss you."

Harlow felt her cheeks burn hot. "And if I dared you, my lord? Would you throw caution to the wind and our reputations and kiss here and now? I would not refuse you," she admitted, hoping he would make a public declaration and soothe her concerns.

He chuckled, but a little of the teasing light left his eyes. "Even if you did dare me, you know I would not. A bachelor's life for me, as you well know, but I think you may have an offer soon, and from a gentleman of whom I, along with your brother-in-law, do not disapprove."

Harlow almost doubled over at the punch that landed in her abdomen. She fought to breathe and stumbled in her steps a moment before recovering. "Really?" she said, her voice far too high. She cleared her throat and tried again. "And who is this gentleman you have picked for me?"

Wes dipped his head toward Lord FitzGeorge, one of the first gentlemen she teased him with at the beginning of their lessons. "FitzGeorge, a baron from Kent."

"Well, I suppose if I have your and Billington's approval, it is all in hand. When he offers I'll be sure to agree," she lied, having no intention of doing so.

Even if she had to slap Wes about the ears to make him realize she was meant for him, she would do as she threatened. What was wrong with the man? Was he so blind that he could not see what was standing right in front of him?

"I think you certainly ought to consider FitzGeorge. He is from a good family with no scandals and I have not heard anything bad concerning how he treats his sisters and staff. You want a love match, and he is looking for one. A romantic, or so Billington has stated."

Harlow stepped out of Wes's arms and stared up at him, aghast. "So you have discussed this with Billington quite profoundly, my lord. You sorted this and that, and all the while, I'm standing over here in the dark until you deem it appropriate to tell me. How very male of you."

Harlow turned and walked away before she said more and did, in fact, clip him over the ears. She felt the tears well up in her eyes, her throat thick, the lump there making it hard to swallow.

She saw a door to the side of the room that servants were walking in and out of and started for it, gaining the shadowy passage just as a hand came about her arm.

"Harlow, what is wrong? I did not mean to upset you by mentioning Lord FitzGeorge. If you do not want to marry him, no one will force you."

She sighed, the fight leaving her and making her knees wobble. "I must sit down." She started for a room adjacent to the door they had just walked through and came into a small, unlit parlor that sat in darkness and unused for the evening.

Harlow slumped onto the settee, hearing the door close and the snick of the lock turning in the bolt.

"You should leave. You do not want to be caught with me. I know how much marriage revolts you." She closed her eyes, hating to say such a thing out loud, but it was true. Even after all the time they had spent together, he still spoke of throwing her off to someone else to marry.

Did he not care even a little?

"That may be so, but you do not. I like you," he said, sitting beside her and taking her hand. "Harlow, what is the matter? Please talk to me."

She raised her eyes to him. Affection and concern shone in his blue depths, and yet she could not bring forth what she wanted to say. Tonight was not the time, but tomorrow was. She would admit all to him when she requested his presence at her sister's house, but well, tonight was for goodbyes. A final farewell, for he would not want anything to do with her when he found out the truth.

"I do not want to talk of marriage, of Lord FitzGeorge or anyone. Just kiss me. Be with me, here and now," she begged, clasping the lapels of his coat and pulling him close.

He stared down at her and watched her, and she could see he was trying to deduce whether she was in earnest or hiding something from him.

"Kiss me, Wes," she begged again before he read her mind. "Kiss me like it's the last time."

HARLOW'S WORDS SENT A BOLT OF PANIC to his gut. *Kiss her like it was the last time?* Hell no, not ever would he accept that. Even if she married, he knew, and to the devil his soul would go, but he would still seduce her to be with him.

If you married her, she could be yours ...

He ignored his voice of reason. The voice that had been becoming louder and louder the more weeks they spent together. Like a clock that ticked with time, counting the hours until she was another man's wife.

He tipped up her chin and kissed her. Hard. There was no softness, no seduction to their embrace. Every brush of their tongues, kisses on lips, jaw, and neck. Each embrace was tainted by panic, an eagerness to have what they both wanted before life got in the way of them being together.

His cock strained against his breeches and she touched him there, taunting him, stroking him until he could bare it no longer. "Turn around," he commanded. "Lift up your skirts."

Her eyes widened, but she did as he asked, leaning on the settee's armrest, watching him over her shoulder. The vision she made, wanton, ready, and eager for him, almost undid him before he could join her.

He ripped open his falls and settled at her back, slipping into her hot, wet heat.

They moaned. Harlow reached back, clasping him about his nape as he thrust inside her. He was already close. His balls ached. Every part of him wanted to spend deep inside her willing cunny.

"Wes," she moaned, tipping her head to the side.

He suckled on her neck, biting and licking her soft, fragrant skin better from his love bites. "I'm going to come, darling," he groaned.

"Me too," she said, just as her contractions tightened about his dick. Her release pulled his own forth, and he spent long and hard into her, milking both their peaks to the very end.

Harlow collapsed into the settee, and he slumped into her back, holding her there for several minutes, their breathing ragged, neither one of them in a rush to leave.

"Will you call on me tomorrow? There is much we need to discuss," she said.

Through her dress, he could feel her heart rate calm. He held his hand there, savoring the feel of her, alive and virile, perfect in every way and in his arms and no one else's.

"I shall call on you after luncheon if that is suitable."

"That will do very well, thank you," she said, turning as much as she could to meet his eye.

Wes took the opportunity to kiss her, not wanting them to return to the ball. Back to reality and life.

If he could, he would stay with her like this forever.

If only he had not promised himself to be a bachelor forever, life in Harlow York's arms would not be so bad after all.

TWENTY-ONE

Harlow paced the parlor on the first floor, only stopping every so often to look out over the gardens and pull her determination together to tell Kemsley the truth.

That she had been using him.

Had lied to him.

There was no choice. She had to say something before another night passed. He had to know that she was in love with him. What her hopes and dreams were, and if he were honest and brave enough to step forward and see that they could make each other happy.

The timing for his call could not be more perfect with her sister and Lord Billington out for a ride in Hyde Park. They would not be back for some time, giving her plenty of opportunity to tell Wes the truth and hopefully gain his forgiveness.

Nerves fluttered in her belly, and she jumped when the butler cleared his throat and announced her guest.

"Lord Kemsley, Miss York," Johnson stated at the door.

She pasted on a welcoming smile and gestured for his lordship to enter. "Thank you, please bring in tea," she ordered before meeting Wes's eyes.

There was mischief there, and she fought to keep her determination and not fall under his wicked spell that she so often did. "Lord Kemsley, thank you for calling on me this afternoon," she said, sitting on a wingback chair that could only fit one person. She did not need him sitting beside her and distracting her.

"I'm happy to be here," he said, waiting for the butler to leave to get the tea. He sat across from her, folding his long legs and reminding her again of how lovely and toned he was. He had muscular thighs, beautiful everything, in truth.

"What is it that you wished to discuss?" he asked her, watching her keenly.

"Well, as to that." She took a fortifying breath. "I think I owe you an explanation, and I'm not certain how you will feel about it after the fact," she said, swallowing her nerves.

"You may tell me whatever you wish. I cannot see whatever it is that you need to tell me that is so very bad, unless ..." His words ran off, and horror replaced his serene visage. "Are you with child?"

Instinctively Harlow clasped her stomach; why, she could not say. "Of course not," she said, having never given it thought—to her chagrin— that she could be. After all they had done together, she supposed it could be a possibility, but her courses were due any day, and she already felt the telltale signs that she would receive menses. "That is not why I asked you here."

The relief that crossed his features left a hollow feeling inside her chest, and her little hope for them crumbled before her. If he did not want children with her, he certainly still did not want marriage.

"Then please, continue," he said as the footman delivered a tray of hot tea and several biscuits.

"Thank you, Johnson. Please leave us now," she ordered. Without prompting, Wes leaned forward and poured them a cup, handing her one before giving her his full attention.

"You were saying," he said.

"I lied to you," Harlow blurted, seeing no other way but to state the truth, as bad as it may sound. "I never had designs on any other gentlemen in the *ton*. I only ever wanted you. I used you to teach me the art of seduction so I may use my wiles on you. Rather successfully, I might add, as much as it shames me to say."

Harlow stared at her cup of tea in her hands, unable to meet Wes's gaze for several moments. She could feel him staring at her, and the quiet stillness that settled over the room told her he was not pleased by her admission.

"Please say something," she whispered, putting down her cup and saucer with a clatter. She did look at him then, and the shock, the betrayal written across his features tore her in two. "I'm sorry, Wes."

"Well, I never," he said after what felt like several hours. "You had me teach you how to kiss, make the most of each dance, suppertimes. By God, I taught you how to eat seductively, and that was all for me. So you may gain my affection and have me as your husband?"

Harlow nodded, forcing down the lump in her throat. "I'm in love with you. I wanted you to be my husband, but you were so determined not to marry that I had to act rashly. I had to make you see me."

"See you, madam?" He stood and strode to the window, staring out at the gardens as she had done earlier. "I thought this was all a game. A little lark before you married the man you loved. Had I known that you loved me and thought I would change my mind, I would never have countered your foolish plan. I would never have given you hope."

Harlow took a deep breath as pain ricocheted

through her like a blow to her person. *He would never have given her hope?*

Which meant she had no hope. Not when it came to them.

"I thought that I may be able to change your mind on that matter. I'm not ashamed to say that I have found you the most interesting, handsome, vexing man since meeting you last Season, and I knew that if I was to have any happiness, I had to try to win your heart. To seduce you. To use your helpful lessons against you was wrong, and I know that, but I did not see any other way forward." Harlow paused, hating how she sounded, how desperate and unhinged she appeared. "I'm sorry. Please forgive me."

WES STARED AT HARLOW AS HIS MIND fumbled and fell over every word she spoke. Her lessons and her need for help were all a ploy. And he had fallen for her pleas like a stupid fool.

"Well, your plan worked. I forget how many times I have bent you over a settee since starting this game, how many times I've snuck into your room and fucked you until we both collapsed from weariness. I cannot believe I have been so stupid, so reckless. I should never have touched you." He turned and faced her, hating her ashen countenance that his words had brought forth, but what did she expect? Did she think he would be happy about being tricked? If he thought her in love with another, he would have let her go, but she wasn't, and he was not sure what to do with that truth now.

"You knew I did not want to marry. That I did not want a wife, not yet and possibly not for some years to come. You have forced my hand, madam."

"I have not forced your hand."

"You could be with a child, and therefore you have. I will not let another man bring up my seed." Wes paused at his own words. When did he start caring about what could transpire? What children he could sire on her? "As careful as we have been, you are still at risk." He shook his head, unable to comprehend the woman he thought he knew could be so callous. So hurtful that she would go against his wishes merely to get her way. "Should your courses not arrive, we shall have to marry. There is no other option. But should you not be with child, I do not ever wish to see you and your lying, scheming self again. I will not be used in such a way. Should the roles be reversed, you know it would be unacceptable for me to treat you in such a way. Mayhap you ought to have thought of that before you made a game of my life to suit your own."

"Wes, I'm sorry."

"Miss York, I'm Lord Kemsley, an earl and your superior in all ways, even morals. Do not speak to me with no honorifics. Today of all days, I cannot stand to hear it."

She shook her head at him, and it only made his blood run hotter. "You have something further to say, Miss York? More schemes and lies that you wish to admit to?" he asked her. She walked over to a nearby settee and stood behind it, holding its back as if for support.

"You are so very grand and superior, are you not? You chastise me for having feelings, for acting on those emotions, and for trying to win what I want most in my life. You." She let out a little laugh, but the sound was far from amusing. "There is no shame in having feelings, my lord. What I feel for you is real and has only grown since we spent time together. Now you may mock me, be angry at me, but do not lie to yourself. You have feelings for me. I know you do, but you refuse to let them shine, to come out into the daylight for everyone to see. You are scared of being hurt. For loving someone when you have never felt those emotions before. I think you feel all those things for me and will not admit it. You're so stubborn and pigheaded, wanting to cling to your bachelor life so much so that you're willing to lose the one thing that is real, tactile, right before you as I am."

Wes stared at her incredulously. He would not stand here and listen to this garbage. He loved his life. His freedom to do as he pleased, and he would not be instructed by a debutante throwing a fit. "You are wrong, madam, in all ways. You are a friend, and I feel for you as much as I feel for Lady Randall or any of the other ladies I have tupped. You are nothing special and should never have thought that you were. Just because you were playing a game and hoping for a conclusion that suited your objective does not mean I shall fall into line because you simply wish it to be so. I do not want a wife. I have been honest with that from the first. I will not marry you unless our escapades have proven fruitful, which we can only hope they have not, for I do not like being played the fool, and our marriage will not be a happy one should I be forced into something I do not want." Wes turned from her and strode toward the door. He needed to leave, get away from her, and the devastation wrought on her pretty face.

This is why he ought not to have helped her. Women were emotional creatures, and that did them credit most of the time, except when it came to him. He had not wanted to hurt her, and had he known of her plan from the beginning, her hopes and dreams, he would never have continued to school her.

Liar. You loved every damn minute in her arms.

He swore, wrenching the door open, ignoring the loud clang as it swung back and hit the wall.

He would not be told what to do, be cornered into a future he did not want, not by Miss York or anyone.

TWENTY-TWO

Harlow did not venture out over the next week, not because she did not want to, but because her menses arrived with a vengeance and killed off the last little hope she had of gaining Lord Kemsley as her husband.

Not that she wanted to marry him under such circumstances or force his hand, and so in a way, she was glad that she was not pregnant. He would never have forgiven her, not that she thought he would even if she were, and to spend years under the same roof, but in a loveless, cold, and fraught marriage would be the worst of torture.

Especially when she still loved him, even after all the hateful words he had said to her.

But what did she expect? She had tricked him, and now he knew it. She would not have been pleased had the roles been reversed, just as he threw at her.

"Come, Harlow, you must rejoin the *ton*. I know you've been poorly this week, but tonight is Viscountess Leigh's ball, and you must attend. Isla is your best friend, and you know she wants you there above anyone else."

Harlow glanced at her sister as she came to sit beside her on the settee. She was in the room of doom, as she now called it, the parlor where Wes had killed all her hopes.

"I will attend, of course, but there is something I need to admit to, and you will be angry with me. Possibly more so than you were last Season when we tricked Lord Billington."

Her sister threw her a dubious look before her features hardened. "I do doubt that. I do not think I could be any angrier at you than I was last year when I had to pretend to be you, but tell me what is troubling you. A problem shared is a problem halved, I've always said."

Harlow lay her head back on the settee and closed her eyes, not sure she wished to see her sister's reaction to what she was about to be told. Harlow told her everything, all her plans, and how she implemented them. How she used what Lord Kemsley taught her against him. She did not tell her that she had been with him intimately; somehow, that seemed wrong, but she did explain how angry he was upon knowing the truth. How unforgiving.

"Harlow, what were you thinking? That is very unkind what you did. I can see how Lord Kemsley may be angry at you."

A lone tear slipped down her cheek, and she swiped it away. "I know, and I apologized, but I think I have lost what little tidbit of his heart I may have held. I'm in love with him, Lila, and he does not feel the same. I thought I could change his mind, but I could not. He was so cold to me, so dismissive. I do not think we can even be friends."

"Oh, my dear." Lila shuffled closer and pulled her into her arms, rubbing her back as their mother used to do when they were little children. "All will be well, Lord Kemsley shall forgive you one day, and you will meet a man worthy of your love. A man who will love you in return even if that gentleman is not Kemsley, I promise you that."

Her sister's words left her stomach in knots. "I do not want anyone but Wes," she admitted, sniffing and attempting to wipe her nose with her hand. "How can I love another when my heart is full with him?"

Her sister sighed, holding her tighter. "You may have to let him go. If Lord Kemsley is determined to remain a bachelor, which is his choice, dearest, there is little you can do about it." Her sister paused, pulling back to meet her eyes. "So long as your interaction with him has not and will not cause you to be ruined, you must try to move on. Your heart in time will heal, for it must if his lordship will not relent. I do not want to see you pining for a man who does not pine for you in return. That is no way to live your life, and you have so much to give. I want to see you married and have children if you're blessed. Be as happy as I am with Billington."

Everything that Harlow had fought for, had wanted, was lost. Kemsley did not want her, and Lila was right. She could not long for a man for the rest of her life. She had such a long life before her. To be pining for one man seemed an awfully sad way to live.

"I will try to heal my heart, I promise, sister. I know it shall not be easy, but nor will I beg his lordship. I gave everything I had to win his heart, and I did not. I will not try again."

"Good, that is what I think too," her sister said, pulling her into a tight embrace.

Harlow reveled in the feel of her sister's arms, strong and comforting. She would need all the support she could gain over the coming weeks. The Season meant her interactions with Kemsley were not over just yet, even if she wished they were.

To see him again would be torture, but one she would endure with aplomb and a chin held high. She would never let him see how much he hurt her, not when he did not care about that fact.

Kemsley lounged on his terrace, glaring at the pink roses that swayed and dropped a few petals on the manicured lawn. For two weeks he had remained home at his rooms at the Albany, refusing all invitations to the Season's events and all because he could not face her.

The Judas.

The liar.

The reckless minx.

Miss Harlow York.

He groaned, downing the last of the brandy he held in his hands. How had he been so blind? How had he fallen for her schemes? Hell, he could have fallen prey to any young, innocent chit who had a wicked and too-quick mind should they have thought to use him in such a way.

That she had not called to notify him that he was to be a father, he could only assume that her courses had arrived and she was not *enceinte*.

The realization gave him no peace. The thought irked him if anything, but he wasn't entirely sure why that was. He was angry, betrayed, but a part of him also wondered what if ...

"My lord, the morning paper has arrived," his butler announced, placing it on the small, round table at his side.

Wes picked it up and read about the upcoming auction at Tattersalls and what the royal family was up to, something about Brighton, before turning to where the banns were called.

"What the goddamn hell," he swore, sitting up in his chair as his eyes flew over the words printed in permanent black ink.

Lord Poulett and Miss Harlow York are to be married four Sundays from today.

Panic assailed him, and a sheen of sweat formed on his skin. For a moment, he thought he might be sick, and he stood, pacing the terrace for several minutes, unsure what to do with himself.

She was betrothed!

To Lord Poulett. Had he not warned her against the cad? What on earth was the chit thinking?

That you do not want her.

Granted, for the past two weeks, he had stayed at home. Only ridden out to Richmond and not Hyde Park so to avoid running into her with her family. The first few days at home, he had reveled in his anger, had cursed her to hell and back, but that soon waned and ebbed into shame.

He could see how she thought her plan was working against him, for if he were to admit the truth, it had been. He did care for her more than he had cared for anyone else, but did he love her?

That he could not say, but now he certainly did not.

Engaged to dandy Poulett. She would have been better off with Lord Hill. Her love was clearly hollow and could not withstand the test of time. Not even two weeks.

He threw down the paper, striding back indoors, yelling out orders for his carriage and valet when he moved to go upstairs. He needed to dress, go and speak to Harlow and find out what the hell she was doing marrying such a man.

She may not be marrying him, but by God, he had warned her against Poulett. Did she learn nothing from their lessons?

It did not take him long to dress, and within ten minutes, the carriage was rocking down Piccadilly heading toward Mayfair.

However, his attempt to call on her was in vain when he was advised that she was out with Lord Poulett. A trip to Hatchards Bookstore was the order of the day.

For several minutes Wes debated going and talking to her there, but he needed to see her without Poulett hovering about, for his words regarding the marquess would not be kind.

Poulett may take offense, and then fisticuffs

may ensue, and he would hate to belt the marquess to a pulp before his betrothed as much as the bastard deserved a bloody nose for even thinking about marrying Harlow.

He returned home, and by the time the evening's entertainment rolled about, his hands shook with the need to see Harlow, to speak to her.

Wes took several long breaths in the carriage as he prepared himself to see her again. It had been two weeks since he found out that she had used him and tried to trick him, but even after all that, he was going to try to stop her from marrying someone else.

Why?

The thought pulled him up short as he alighted from the carriage. A footman in navy liveried apparel took his top hat and gloves before he moved into the ballroom. Several acquaintances greeted him, and he stopped to speak to them, biding his time until his prey came into view.

And then she did ...

The kick to his heart startled him, and he snapped his mouth closed, not wanting to look like a gaping dog drooling over a juicy bone.

Not that Harlow was a juicy bone, but she was beautiful tonight, by God. Prettier than he had ever seen her before.

No, that was not true. She had always been beautiful. The only difference now was she wasn't smiling up at him anymore, but someone else entirely.

Poulett.

TWENTY-THREE

Without seeing Lord Kemsley, she knew he was here at the ball. Her body sensed his presence, her skin prickled, and her heart beat irregularly at the thought of seeing him again.

She did not want to see him. To be reminded of what she had lost.

You cannot lose what you did not have, Harlow...

She nodded, agreeing with herself even though she never spoke the words aloud. She glanced about, hoping no one saw or was interested in her, and they were not.

The Season's diamond Miss Sweeney had become engaged overnight to Lord Abercromby, and the *ton* was all aflutter with congratulations and happy remarks to the couple who were in attendance with their parents.

Lord Abercromby stood at her side. His lofty

stance and severe nose that he looked down on everyone with told Harlow he was proud to win her hand. She supposed that his life would not change all that much besides getting his hands on Miss Sweeney's dowry, he ought to be pleased.

As for herself and her engagement to Lord Poulett, Harlow could not help but wonder if she had acted in haste. Saying yes to the marquess had been a way to prove to Lord Kemsley that no matter her feelings, she could move forward from him without nary a look back.

How wrong she was.

"Come, my dear. Shall we dance?" Lord Poulett asked, holding out his arm.

Harlow nodded, letting him lead her out onto the dance floor. Two other couples joined them, and the breath in her lungs seized when Lord Kemsley joined their set with Lady Randall.

She should know that the Lady Randall, his old lover, would be whom he ran back to after their short time together. She fought for calm, tried not to glare at either of them and failed miserably.

Lady Randall's knowing smirk irked Harlow further, and for several seconds, she wanted to harm her ladyship physically. Instead, she stood, holding hands with Lord Poulett and another gentleman at her other side she did not know, and took a deep, calming breath.

Violence, no matter in what form, was not warranted.

The first notes of the dance commenced, and they were soon weaving, joining other partners through the steps. Unfortunately, just as her serendipity was going these days, she was partnered with Lord Kemsley.

The moment his arms slipped behind her back, her hand held firmly in his, everything that they had shared, all the times they talked, the many kisses and touches, the laughter overwhelmed her, and an emptiness swamped her, knowing she would no longer have what they shared.

Certainly not with her betrothed, who tolerated her at best, liked her somewhat, but more than that, and she would be deluding herself.

"What do you think you're playing at marrying Lord Poulett? I warned you about him, and you agreed to be his wife! What were you thinking, Harlow?" he asked her under his breath, but she heard the warning, the anger in his tone.

"What does it matter to you what I do? I must marry someone. I will not go into a third Season like some tragic debutante who cannot find a husband."

He glared down at her as she glared up at him. "You have a lot of nerve, Lord Kemsley schooling me on what I should and should not do. Are you not here with Lady Randall? You ran back to her skirts quick enough." Harlow fought not to let jealousy get the better of her but failed miserably. She was jealous, angry, heartbroken, and betrothed to a man she did not love, nor like.

Everything she had hoped for had turned to dust.

"Excuse us a moment," he said to their dancing partners before taking her arm and dragging her from the ballroom floor. She wrenched her arm back, unwilling to let him think he could control her.

"Come with me, Harlow. We must talk."

She crossed her arms over her chest, not moving an inch. "You had two weeks to come and speak to me, and you did not. When you did not even bother to call on me to find out if I had ...if I had ..." Harlow could not say the words.

"When you did not send word, I assumed ... that there was no need for me to call on you."

"And yet you think you can pull me from a dance and scold me over my choice of husband. You did not want the position, my lord. Have you forgotten or failed to understand that by having such a stance, you lose any ability to tell me what to do? Not that I would allow you to in any case."

"He has a mistress, and from what I know of him, he will not give her up."

Harlow gestured toward Lady Randall. "It seems he is not the only gentleman in London who will not give up their lovers. Tell me I am wrong?" she asked him, raising her brow.

The man was infuriating and so handsome when in high temper that her body wanted to defy her and go to him. Wrap herself up in all his strength and masculinity and revel in it one more time.

But she could not. He did not want her. He clearly wanted Lady Randall and the life he was so fond of before meeting her.

The very thought made her want to cast up her accounts.

"I can see from your stubborn countenance that you would not believe me even if I were to deny the charge."

"You are right," she said. "I would not believe a word you say."

"Just as I will not believe a word you say since you're so very good at keeping secrets and playing tricks on people you claim to care about."

She gasped, feeling his barb sharp and hard to her heart. "I will not apologize again." She stepped closer to him, not wanting to draw any more attention to themselves than they were already bringing. "I wanted you," she whispered. "I wanted you as my husband, my lover, the father of my children. Granted, I should not have played my games, but what else was I to do? What other ways should I have caught your attention, had your presence near me these many weeks? A lady cannot go out to gaming hells on her own. I could not go to your club and enjoy a wine with you or call on you at your home. I asked for your help, hoping you would see what was before you and maybe pierce a little of your heart. But I was wrong. You have no heart, and you feel nothing. Not for anyone."

Harlow shook her head. This argument was not necessary, nor was this the place to have more heated discussions. "I must move on with my life. Try to find happiness and marry Lord Poulett. I'm sure after I give him a son he will be happy enough to leave me alone. I can be content living with the love of my children if not my husband. It is done, Lord Kemsley, and nothing can change my choice. Not even your misplaced lectures from a man who did not want a say in my life. Who chose another path when the opportunity has arisen."

The fight left Harlow. "Goodbye, Kemsley, and good wishes for your future."

WES WATCHED HARLOW TURN AND WALK away, and fear seized his heart. "I made a mistake," he shouted across the room. The musicians halted their playing, and all eyes turned upon them, wide and eager to see more.

He did not care what they heard or saw. He

could not let her go. Could not let her marry a man she did not love.

He could not allow her to marry anyone but him.

She turned, her eyes as wide as everyone else's. Wes was sure not a sound in Mayfair could be heard just so his next words would be audible.

She did not ask him what he meant, merely stared at him, waiting for his pride, his determination to ignore how she made him feel to fall.

"You cannot marry Poulett," he declared, ignoring the gasps.

Poulett stormed over to be beside Harlow, his small hand pointing in his direction. "You cannot say that, Kemsley. Who do you think you are?"

Wes disregarded Poulett's words, mayhap knowing for the first time in his life who he was and what he wanted. "I read in the paper today your betrothal announcement, and I knew I had to see you. To tell you, Harlow York, that you cannot marry Poulett or anyone who has been courting you this Season."

"And why is that?" she asked him finally, the tremor in her voice giving him hope.

"Because, Miss York, you must marry me," he declared, wanting to reach out and pull her into his arms. Hold her, kiss her, promise her the world and everything in it. Beg for forgiveness for being obstinate and unfeeling.

She bit her lip, her eyes filling with unshed

tears, and Poulett took a menacing step toward him.

"Now see here, she's my fiancée. I have spent many hours courting her, and she has picked me over you, Kemsley."

"Go back to your mistress, Poulett. Miss York will not abide by a husband who is not faithful. Not like I shall be and promise to be should she agree to be my wife."

"Oh, Wes," she whispered.

He closed the space between them, brushing her tears away with his fingers.

Poulett went to throw him off, and Kemsley thrust him aside and was thankful to see Billington step up to them and usher the marquess away, his many admonitions breaking the room's silence.

Harlow giggled, her eyes bright with hope.

"Marry me, Harlow York. I'm sorry for being so blind to how you made me feel. I was so determined to ignore my feelings that I almost lost you. But I promise, from this day forward, I will never push you aside again. You have my heart, and I cannot live without it. Without you."

She stepped into his hold, and he wrenched her against him, reveling in the feel of her in his arms. "Marry me," he whispered again, leaning his forehead on hers. "Marry me, Harlow. You're the love of my life, my everything. Please be mine."

Her smile made his heart sing, and she nodded, reaching up to clasp him about his nape. "Yes, Lord Kemsley, my heart, my love. I will marry you," she said.

Unlike any he had ever known, happiness burst through him, and without thought, he closed the space between them and kissed her. He ignored the scandalous outbursts, they would deal with that scandal tomorrow, but for tonight he would kiss his wife-to-be.

Seal their love, their future with a kiss and the disgrace be damned. He wasn't a rogue for nothing. In times like these, that title came in handy.

Epilogue

1815 Stonelake Manor, Kent

Harlow stood beside Wes as their eldest son, now three, and his younger sister, just twelve months, played on the two ponies the Dowager Countess of Kemsley had gifted them this past Christmas.

They would soon return to town for the upcoming Season, and Harlow was filled with trepidation and excitement. She would be sponsoring her cousin, Miss Sophie York, from the small village of Highclere. It had been several years since she had seen her cousin, but her aunt, who had fallen on hard times, had written, begging her to help, and she could not refuse.

"Are you sure you wish to travel to London this year, my dear? I know leaving the children behind will be hard. We do not have to go if you do not want to," Wes said, watching her keenly.

During the past four years of marriage, they had grown even closer than they were when he declared himself before all the *ton*. A scandalous event she was certain would ruin them, but the matrons, instead of shunning them, fell for Lord Kemsley's charms that evening and declared the fall of a rake was an event to celebrate, not rebuke.

"I will be fine. The children will be here with your mama and their nannies. They will not miss us too much, and we can return mid-Season if we need. Aunt Agnes wrote and said Sophie was a beauty, and with our connections, I'm sure we can find her a good match."

Wes nodded, keeping his attention on his children. "Not too fast, Frederick," he called out, the groom leading their son, pulling the horse into a slower walk.

Harlow bit back a grin. For all his determination to remain a bachelor, her husband had taken to marriage and fatherhood rather well, better than she had adjusted if she were honest. Becoming the lady of great estates and multiple servants was difficult, and she floundered a little at the beginning. Had it not been for her dearest mother-in-law, she may not have survived at all.

"When is Miss York due to arrive?" Wes asked her.

"Any moment now," Harlow said, just as the rumbling of an approaching carriage sounded through the old oaks lining their drive.

Harlow took Wes's arm, and they started toward the house, wanting to greet their house guest. Harlow had written to Sophie over the past few months, and she felt as though she knew her a little and hoped she would have a successful Season.

They made the front doors as the carriage rolled to a halt, and a footman ran out to open the door and let down the step. A young woman, hair as light as her husband and large blue eyes, came into view, and Harlow gaped.

She was utterly stunning. Harlow turned to Wes, only to find him grinning as if he was thinking the same. That this Season she would have her hands full. Not with invitations and dresses and everything that came with sponsoring a young woman, but keeping the many gentlemen from breaking down their doors.

She jumped down from the carriage, dipping into a curtsy that needed a little work, if Harlow was being honest.

"Lady Kemsley, Lord Kemsley, thank you so much for having me," Sophie said, smiling.

"You are very welcome," Wes said, coming up to Harlow's side. "Good luck, my dear. I fear you will have a very busy Season indeed."

Harlow waved his concerns aside, turning

back to her cousin. "It is lovely to meet you in person finally," she said, moving to take Sophie's hand. "Please call me Harlow, and his lordship Kemsley."

"Of course," Sophie said, her attention moving to the house. "Gah, your home is immense," she said. "As big as Highclere."

Harlow smiled, and Wes kissed her cheek. "I shall attend the children and leave you to your cousin. Have fun, my love," he whispered, winking at her.

Harlow watched him stride away, her gaze moving to his muscular thighs in his buckskin breeches, his taut bottom hers to admire from this position.

"Are all the gentlemen in London as handsome as the earl? I think the Season will be eventful indeed if it is," Sophie said, not taking her attention off the house.

Harlow took a deep breath and linked her arm with her cousin, moving them inside. "He was a hard gentleman to catch, but with my help, I'm sure we can find one just like him to suit you. There is nothing I like more than a good plan to hook rakes, and I have many."

Sophie grinned, her mouth agape as she entered the foyer of the Kemsley ancestral home. A similar reaction to what Harlow had when she first viewed it.

"A plan? Do you mean antics, my lady?" she asked with a mischievous tone. "I do love a good intrigue."

Harlow chuckled, moving them upstairs. "As do I, Sophie. As do I."

Thank you for taking the time to read *My Reckless Earl*! I hope you enjoyed the seventh book in my Wayward Woodvilles series!

I'm forever grateful to my readers, and if you're able, I would appreciate an honest review of *My Reckless Earl*. As they say, feed an author, leave a review!

Alternatively, you can keep in contact with me by visiting my website, subscribing to my newsletter or following me online. You can contact me at www.tamaragill.com.

Tamara Gill

Don't Miss Tamara's Other Romance Series

The Wayward Yorks

A Wager with a Duke

My Reformed Rogue

Wild, Wild, Duke

The Wayward Woodvilles

A Duke of a Time

On a Wild Duke Chase

Speak of the Duke

Every Duke has a Silver Lining

One Day my Duke Will Come

Surrender to the Duke

My Reckless Earl

Brazen Rogue

The Notorious Lord Sin

Wicked in My Bed

Royal House of Atharia

To Dream of You

A Royal Proposition

Forever My Princess

League of Unweddable Gentlemen

Tempt Me, Your Grace

Hellion at Heart

Dare to be Scandalous

To Be Wicked With You

Kiss Me, Duke

The Marquess is Mine

Kiss the Wallflower

A Midsummer Kiss

A Kiss at Mistletoe

A Kiss in Spring

To Fall For a Kiss

A Duke's Wild Kiss

To Kiss a Highland Rose

Lords of London

To Bedevil a Duke

To Madden a Marquess

To Tempt an Earl

To Vex a Viscount

To Dare a Duchess

To Marry a Marchioness

To Marry a Rogue

Only an Earl Will Do

Only a Duke Will Do

Only a Viscount Will Do

Only a Marquess Will Do

Only a Lady Will Do

A Time Traveler's Highland Love

To Conquer a Scot

To Save a Savage Scot

To Win a Highland Scot

A Stolen Season

A Stolen Season

A Stolen Season: Bath

A Stolen Season: London

Scandalous London

A Gentleman's Promise

A Captain's Order

A Marriage Made in Mayfair

High Seas & High Stakes

His Lady Smuggler

Her Gentleman Pirate

A Wallflower's Christmas Wreath

Daughters Of The Gods

Banished

Guardian

Fallen

Stand Alone Books

Defiant Surrender

A Brazen Agreement

To Sin with Scandal

Outlaws

About the Author

Tamara is an Australian author who grew up in an old mining town in country South Australia, where her love of history was founded. So much so, she made her darling husband travel to the UK for their honeymoon, where she dragged him from one historical monument and castle to another.

A mother of three, her two little gentlemen in the making, a future lady (she hopes) keep her busy in the real world, but whenever she gets a moment's peace she loves to write romance novels in an array of genres, including regency, medieval and time travel.